Praise for Janie's Hope

"S.R. Fabrico seamlessly weaves the tale of Janie's Hope together with her captivating story-telling and rich characters that you both intrinsically love and loathe for the duration. A true nail-biter that keeps you guessing until the very end, Janie's Hope is a must read."

~Brook Plack, Navigating Personal Growth Podcast

"I felt quite sad and nostalgic while reading Janie's Hope because I know that it is the last book of this captivating series. I think Janie's Hope is the perfect conclusion to the Southport Series and I even had a big smile on my face when I was finished. The very first page of the book had my attention and it didn't let go until the very end and even then I was still pondering it long after. I have loved every book in the series but this one is my favorite, Janie's Hope is an enchanting story."

~Leanne, Bookstagrammer – Leanne Reads and Reviews

"Keeping Janie is what romantic suspense dreams are made of...keeps you on your toes with unpredictable plot twists that have you begging for the next book."

@toriannharris, Book Tok

"S.R. Fabrico really outdid herself with this one. Keeping Janie is an intense masterpiece that you will not be able to put down."

~J. Lane, Avid Reader

"The mystery at the book's heart is revealed in layers, surprising reader's with the story's depth. Call Her Janie is a fantastic selection for readers who enjoy deep mysteries with friends-to-lovers romance."

~C. Hoyle, Reader's Favorite 5-Star Review

"Call Her Janie is a page-turning novel. The plot was brilliantly planned and executed, and I was intrigued by the story."

~A. Boucher, Reader's Favorite 5-Star Review

Also by S.R. Fabrico

Fiction:

The Secrets We Conceal

Call Her Janie

Keeping Janie

Janie's Hope

Ten Thousand Steps

Non Fiction:

The Pioneers of All Star

My Firefly Journal

My Cheer Journal

My Dance Journal

My Gymnastics Journal

My Soccer Journal

My Swim Journal

My Basketball Journal

My Volleyball Journal

My Crew Journal

Janie's Hope

Book 3 of the Southport Series

S.R. Fabrico

Mia,
Laugh often!
S.R. Fabrico
1/24/25

SRF Creations

This book is a work of Oction. Any reference to historical events, real people, or real places are used Octionally. 'ther names, characters, places, and events are products of the authorHs imagination, and any resemblance to actual events or places or persons, living or dead, is entirely coincidental.

Paperback ISBN – Amazon 978-1-962546-07-2

Paperback ISBN – Ingram 978-1-962546-09-6

Hard Cover ISBN – Amazon 978-1-962546-08-9 $25.99

For Avery and Jon,

Chase your dreams, live life to the fullest, and be kind.

Love, Mom

Janie's Hope

PROLOGUE

Counting the tiny holes in the drop ceiling, I waited for the news no one ever wanted to hear. Time crept by as anticipation draped over me like a thousand-pound cloak. All the money in the world couldn't buy my immortality. I stared at the poster-sized frames of the human body's anatomy that hung on the walls. My focus blurred. Deep in my gut, I suspected the Grim Reaper planned to visit me. My days were numbered. As my vision came back into focus, I read the signs taped to the door promoting the newest pharmaceutical drug and laughed at the litany of side effects.

Finally, the knock came.

Dr. Fine entered the room. His gray hair seemed unkept like he had just run his fingers through the delicate strands on his head. He pulled a pen from his coat pocket and used the tip to tap the screen on his iPad. He dropped his head as he wiped his hand down his tie and cleared his throat before he spoke.

"Well, Gray," he said, "I'm sorry I don't have good news for you today."

"Just hit me with it, Doc."

"You have stage four lung cancer."

I think I spaced out for a few minutes. Staring at the cirrocumulus clouds through the narrow window helped me feel less claustrophobic. I took several deep breaths, which sent me into a full-blown coughing fit.

"At this stage, there isn't much we can do. There's a new experimental treatment you could try. I can begin testing today to see if you're a candidate. I can prescribe medicine to keep you comfortable. You can also do nothing, which I don't recommend."

"How long do I have?" I hung my head and sighed.

"Worst case, three months. Best case, maybe six to nine months. You'll most likely get worse. Do you have someone who can help you?"

"I don't want anyone to know."

Dr. Fine shook his head in disapproval, his shoulders rising and falling in a slight shrug. "I don't think that's a wise decision."

"It's not your decision to make," I said, coughing profusely as I gasped for air.

"Take some time to think everything over. I encourage you to get a second and third opinion. I can recommend a pulmonologist in Billings." He pulled the pen back out of his pocket and wrote a few names on a piece of paper. "These are some colleagues of mine. They are great doctors. Maybe they'll have a different opinion."

I slid off the table and said, "Thank you."

My limbs were numb. *I'm fucking Gray Stone. I'm not dying. I will not accept this fate.*

ONE

Hope

Glancing in my rearview mirror, I spotted a black SUV. *Was that the same black SUV behind me a few miles back?* I put my blinker on and changed lanes. I waited. A few seconds later, the black SUV followed. *What's this douchebag doing? Why is he following me?* I counted to two hundred and changed lanes again, gently moving my car into the far-left lane. I counted again, one, two, three, four. This time, I reached one thousand before the black sedan followed. He was clearly trying to be discreet and create distance between us. *The joke's on you, asshole. I've been trained to spot you.*

My father, billionaire Gray Stone, didn't allow me to go into public without pointing out every exit and every person who appeared even *slightly* suspicious. He liked to make a game out of situation awareness. Sometimes, he'd plant people to be my attackers.

He'd say, "Hope, you must pay attention to your surroundings. You must spot those things that are hiding in plain sight."

To win the game, I'd have to figure out who the culprits were and escape. Keith, our bodyguard, once pretended to follow us when my father and I headed into town. I was too young to drive then, but my father made me give him instructions on how to get away.

The black SUV was tucked a few cars behind mine in the left lane. At the last minute, I jerked the Land Rover across all three lanes of traffic onto the exit ramp. The black SUV darted across the highway and skid just in time to reach the exit, making it clear that he was, in fact, following me. I turned left at the light and did my best to weave through the cars before yanking the Rover into a U-turn in the middle of the road and pulling back onto the highway. My U-turn caused a bit of a traffic jam, leaving Mr. Douchebag in the black SUV blocked. With a not-so-friendly gesture, I raised my favorite finger as I cruised past him. The interior of his vehicle remained hidden, but that didn't matter to me. My main focus was to increase the distance between us. The engine roared to life as I slammed my foot down on the accelerator, burning rubber and racing down the road.

The highway stretched out flat and dry as far as I could see. Cruising, I jammed to the oldies as Blinding Lights blared on the radio. The wind blew my hair back as it burst through the open windows on my gently pre-owned Land Rover. By pre-owned,

I mean, it was my father's old ranch vehicle. My sandy-blond hair, which I got from my father, flew around my head. The breeze slapped my face as the sun beat through the windshield and charged my soul. Oddly, my heartbeat pumped faster, and my muscles tightened as I drove.

At almost twenty-three years old, I left the comfort of home for the first time. The slightest bit of guilt trickled into my stomach. *I should have told my father I was leaving and where I was going.* I shook my head. *No, he wouldn't have let me go.*

My father made sure I traveled the world through books and was exceptionally well educated, but I spent my life with him on our ranch in Montana. He did his best to ensure I had everything I needed, yet I couldn't shake the desire to spread my wings and soar. The world called me by name. Ready or not, I was charging into my future like a dog in hot pursuit of his bone.

"Southport changed everything, Hope." My father's words fluttered through my mind. My mother died when I was a little girl. I longed to be close to her as far back as I could remember. I longed to meet her family and explore the town she and my father loved. I longed to know her in any way possible.

According to my father, Southport, North Carolina, was an incredible place. He said that the town and its residents changed him into a good man worthy of being my father. He described a beautiful white house with a bright red roof on the water's edge. He said my mother and I lived in that house with her husband, Josh Miller. "Josh loved you like you were his daughter."

My father didn't have photographs of our family from Southport. "It's too dangerous to have any connection to our past," he had told me. The phrase echoed in my mind. My lips curled into a smile as memories of my father's bedtime stories popped into my head. Night after night, I learned stories about Uncle Randy, Aunt Renee, Helen, and her bookstore. In great detail, my father described each of their personalities, including Josh's. I especially loved hearing about the house with the red roof and Bayview Books, where my mom worked. My last name was Miller because my mom would have wanted it that way. "Miller's a common name," my father had said. "No one will suspect it has any connection to our past."

Darkness crept into the sky as the sun began to set. *Welcome to Tennessee*, the sign read as the white letters reflected off my headlights. Feeling safe, I took the next exit and pulled into a gas station. I was starving and had to pee like a stallion. As I approached the convenience store door, a white and brown spotted doodle dog, the size of a German shepherd, greeted me with her paw. I recognized the breed from a book I read back on the ranch. She sat on her hind legs, raised her paw, and tapped my arm.

"Well, hello there, little doggy," I said, doing the pee-pee dance. She cupped her paw around my arm. "Okay, okay. I need to go inside now." I squirmed and brushed her paw off as I entered the store.

Squeezing my thighs together, I raced toward the bathroom and unzipped my pants along the way. I burst into an available stall, struggled with the paper toilet seat cover, and nearly collapsed onto the toilet. "Ahhh."

While I washed my hands at the sink, a girl dressed entirely in orange appeared beside me. Her spongy, perfectly curled, bleach-blond hair cascaded down her back. Her face was perfectly painted, and her long, thick lashes fluttered as she assessed me from head to toe. A sense of pity flickered in her eyes as she took in my appearance.

"Do I know you?" I said flatly.

"Oh, heavens no," she said in a soft Southern drawl.

"Well, you were looking at me like you might know me." I pressed my feet firmly into the ground and puffed my chest out.

"Bless your heart," the girl said with a Southern twang. She wadded up her paper towel and threw it into the trash can. "You have a good night, now, ya hear." She closed the door behind her.

What the hell? *Blessing my heart.* I should have drop-kicked that bitch and stuffed her and her orange outfit into the toilet. What's a Tennessee Vol, anyway?

A burly man, whose name tag read Bo, rang up my purchase. I smiled and waved as I left the store and made my way to the Land Rover. The happy, tail-wagging doodle dog was in the backseat, with her head hanging out the window.

"What on earth?" I said as I opened the back door. "Out, dog. Out." I pointed to the pavement.

The dog scooted farther back into the Rover and refused to exit. She let out a little whimper and then a yelp.

"You can't come with me. You have to get out." I grabbed the nape of her neck and pulled. She slid like a corpse across the back seat. I pulled her out of the car, and the dog whined as her paws hit the pavement. "Bye, doggy. Good girl." I patted her on the head and shut the door.

I nestled into the driver's seat and fired up the Land Rover. As I slowly drove away, I saw the doodle dog in my rearview mirror chasing the car. The next thing I knew, she flew through the air, jumping at the window.

"Seriously?" I slammed on the brakes. She raised her paw in the air and barked. "Ugh!" I sighed, but her puppy dog eyes pierced my heart. I flung open the door. "Come on, pup. Hop in!" I said, a bit unwillingly. The dog tilted her head and placed her paw gently on my arm. She bounded over me and settled into the back seat, looking up at me with the most sorrowful and endearing gaze.

I groaned and let out a breath. "You're going to get in the way," I said sternly. The dog covered her eyes with her paws. I threw my hands into the air. "I guess you can hitch a ride." I pointed my finger at her. "I can't have a dog. I don't even know where I'm staying. Do you understand? Just a ride. That's all."

She lay down, raised her eyebrows one at a time, yawned, and relaxed in the backseat.

TWO

Hope

"Dog, you stink." I was grateful for the company, although the stench was less than desired.

The dog groaned and rested her head on the back of my seat. Her breath was heavy on my neck as she sighed.

"What's your name, anyway? You must have a name."

The dog sat on her hind legs and stared into the rearview mirror.

"Is it Penny?" Nothing. "Is it Queenie?" Nothing. "Is it Judy?"

The dog growled, and I laughed. "I take it you don't like Judy." After twenty more guesses, we got nowhere. "I'll call you DD for doodle dog."

The dog didn't seem to mind the name. I moved my bag and motioned for her to hop into the front seat. She obliged and then performed about fifty circles until she found the right spot to lie down. Her puppy dog eyes looked up at me, and my heart melted.

"My father always said I had the emotions of a robot, except when it came to animals." I rubbed my hand across her snout. "I think I'm just logical, and humans are complicated. Animals are simple. You know what I mean, DD?"

She lifted her head, adjusted her paws, and put her head back down.

"Exactly, DD. You get it. Dogs are loyal. Innocent. What's not to love?"

We rode in silence for a bit while DD slept. The quiet was therapeutic. Without distraction, my mind could wander to the many great places I've read about in my books. On the other hand, the silence could be deafening and even terrifying. Being alone with my thoughts wasn't always healthy for me.

"DD. You awake?"

She groaned and forced open one eye about halfway.

"I'm anxious."

She yawned a gigantic yawn and slowly pulled herself to a sitting position. She raised her paw and tilted her head. Then she took the tip of her nose and used it to flick my hand on top of her head.

I laughed. "You want me to pet you?" I rubbed her head, and her tail wagged furiously, beating against the passenger side window.

I looked at DD. "My father told me stories about my mother and her family. I feel like I know them, but the truth is, I don't know them at all."

DD rested her head on the center console and placed her paw on my wrist.

"I don't remember my mother." I sighed. "Is it weird to miss someone you didn't know or can't remember?"

She sat up and let out a little squawk like a bird.

"My heart has always had this little ache inside. A constant tiny pain that won't go away."

Her eyes looked soulful and intense as if she understood what I was saying.

"Sometimes I wonder if I miss my mother or the idea of having a mother." I turned the radio down so DD could hear what I was saying better. "I want to find my mother's husband. I guess he was kind of like my father, too. I can't imagine having two. The one I have is plenty." I laughed. DD flicked my hand again with her nose, this time rolling over so I could pet her neck and chest.

"My father thinks the world's too dangerous for me. What do you think, DD? I want to feel close to my mother. I want to find myself. On the other hand, I have enough money for you and me to find a little cabin in the woods. Wouldn't that be nice?"

DD started to howl and turned to face the window. She pressed her nose against the glass in a huff.

"Okay. Okay. No cabin. Besides, you're just getting a ride, anyway. Once I get where I'm going, you're on your own, remember?"

She used her paw to push the window button and stuck her head out. Her tongue flapped in the wind as saliva smacked the back window.

"Fine, DD. Be that way. I guess you don't want any treats. That's your choice."

She turned to look at me with her nose in the air and snapped her head back out the window.

THREE

Hope

As I approached Southport, tall hotels and condominium buildings stood tall on either side of the road. The town seemed to contradict my father's description. As I ventured towards the intercoastal waterway, Southport's downtown unfolded before me, as charming and delightful as my father had promised.

Towering oak trees with grand trunks flanked the road on either side. Their branches arched gracefully over the street, providing a canopy to protect everything from the sun beneath its veil. Families and friends beamed with smiles and laughter as they frolicked along the sidewalks. Golf carts and bicycles buzzed by. The scene was intoxicating. Waves of emotions crashed over me, filling my heart with joy while simultaneously choking me. I had never experienced a surge of emotions quite like this before.

Montana was beautiful, and I loved our ranch, but I had never experienced this many happy people living side by side like a tiny secret community. According to my father, reality and everyday life slowly poisoned the rest of the world, but Southport was a sanctuary of epic proportions.

I turned the Land Rover left onto Bay Street and crawled along the road, admiring the barge passing through the waterway. I inhaled deeply, and the smell of salt water graced my nose. Instantly, a peaceful calm washed over me. *This is what the sea smells like.* Dr. Emoto was right in his book *The Hidden Messages In Water.* He understood a human being's connection to water, and now I understood it, too.

In the distance, I spotted a splash of red through the trees. My peaceful calm evaporated as my heartbeat quickened with each passing second as I edged closer to the house with the red roof.

Josh Miller's home.

The very place where I spent my early childhood with my mother and the man of her dreams. My father painted him as the perfect husband and father. Truly the kind of man that every girl fantasizes about but seldom encounters. If I didn't know better, I'd think my father had a crush on Josh.

I inhaled until I couldn't suck in any more breath, closed my eyes, and exhaled. DD turned toward me, yawned, and let out a little squeak. She lifted her paw and set it on top of my arm. "I know, girl. I'm sorry we fought, too."

Her puppy dog eyes stared at me and then looked toward the house.

A pristine white sign in the front yard with shiny gold letters read Waylen Miller House. I drove slowly up the driveway and put the car in park. Small black letters traced the bottom of the sign, reading *Museum of Southport*, monitored by the Historical Society.

Five minutes ago, I wasn't entirely sure I wanted to meet Josh Miller, and now a painful ache filled my heart as I clutched my chest in an effort to create more space for my heart to beat.

"How can this be?" I said to DD as a small tear fell from my eye. I wiped it away immediately, sniffed, and cleared my throat. "I am Hope Miller, and Hope Miller doesn't cry." I reached over to pet DD on the head, but she was gone. I slumped back into my seat.

Figures. The damn dog just used me for a ride.

Startled by loud barking and growling, I exited the car to find DD perched on the house's doorstep. Standing on the massive front porch, she looked quite small. She jumped in circles, wagged her tail, and started barking again. She barked at the door like it was going to attack us.

"DD, stop. Stop that right now." I pointed toward the car. "Get back in the car." She continued barking loudly. "DD, enough. Get in the car."

My back was towards the door, facing the street, as a muffled voice said, "Sorry, we're closed today."

I turned around and waved my arms in the air as I hollered through the door. "No, no, I'm sorry. My dog has a mind of her own. I didn't mean to bother you. Have a nice day."

DD was jumping and scratching at the door, and I tried to calm her down as the door flung open. A bald, somewhat older man stood in the doorway to the beautiful historic house. He wore green sweatshorts, a red sweater covered in flashing Christmas lights, and blue French hen socks. I stood in shock, unsure of what to say. Christmas had thrown up on this man.

"Hello. The museum is closed today."

DD suddenly sat perfectly still beside me and raised a paw as if she planned to shake the man's hand.

"You mentioned that." I swiped at DD's paw and pushed it down. "We'll be on our way."

The man fixed his gaze on me. His brown eyes froze, ensnaring me in a single, intense moment. For an instant, I thought I might need to chop his throat and run.

His shoulders drooped slightly, and I sensed he was a docile man. "I'm here with my family, decorating the museum for Christmas. Our good friend is the president of the Historical Society. We're helping her out."

I chewed my bottom lip and considered if I should ask about Josh. I didn't care about the house. I was looking for my stepfather.

"I'd be glad to give you a tour," he said, opening the door wide and waving his arm for me to enter. Something about this bald man and the intensity of his gaze set my senses on high alert.

The interior of the house resembled Santa's Village. At least a dozen boxes had garland and lights spewing out of the tops, and glitter sparkled in every nook and cranny.

"Excuse the mess. As I said, we're decorating for Christmas." He offered his hand for a shake and said, "My name's Randy."

FOUR

Hope

My mind was utterly confused, and my heart wanted to beat straight out of my chest. As I stepped through the threshold, I couldn't help but wonder if I would find my stepfather inside. The man who introduced himself as Randy reached out his hand. His skin was calloused, and his grip was firm.

"Hi. I'm Hope," I said as I sized him up. My mom's brother was named Randy, but I had no way of knowing if this was my uncle.

A commotion stirred from another room. A woman with long, dark hair knotted into a braid rounded the corner. She froze in her tracks when she saw me.

"This is my wife, Renee," Randy said. His tone sounded polite, but he was covering something. "She startles easily." He laughed nervously.

I nodded and smiled. *What are the chances that there would be another married couple named Randy and Renee? Could this be my aunt and uncle?*

"Is that your dog?" Renee asked. Her mouth barely moved, her eyes were wide as saucers, and her neck began to turn a splotchy red.

Shaking my head, I said, "She sort of hopped into my car during my trip and hasn't left."

Randy and Renee led me toward the kitchen. DD followed behind.

"I've been traveling across the country for several days." I patted the dog's head. "DD's been good company."

Renee stood rigidly, unable to move. "DD?"

I concentrated on my breathing. *Be cool, be cool. Breathe normally. Do they recognize me?*

"Yes, DD. Short for Doodle dog." I shifted my weight and said, "I came here looking for the owner of this house." The hair on my arms began to stand erect as I realized I could be standing in the very kitchen where my mother was murdered by the woman who kidnapped me. *Twice.*

Renee stood as still as a statue. Her skin glistened as a streak of light peeked through the window.

"We know, Josh," Randy replied. "But he mostly keeps to himself these days." I felt my heart race, a tightness building in my chest as I fought to maintain my expression. Clenching my fists at my sides, I focused on the ground, determined not to let my emotions show. "We can show you around the house if you'd like."

They seemed oblivious to who I was, or perhaps they knew exactly who I was and were choosing to conceal it for some reason. I was grappling with my thoughts to figure out which. A part of me wanted to shout, "Hey, I'm your niece," but I wasn't sure I was ready yet. I don't know why. I came here to meet my family, but in my head, I was going to start with Josh.

Randy and Renee led me into the living room. My eyes widened as I took in the room. A giant fourteen-foot Christmas tree stood in the corner. As we entered, a red-haired young woman and a nerdy, yet adorable, guy around my age were placing glittering gold curly sprigs into the tree. Surrounded by boxes of gold ornaments and matching bows, the girl delicately navigated her way toward us.

"What do you think?" she said with a huge smile stretched across her face.

Randy cleared his throat. "Hope, this is our daughter, Ava," he said, opening his arm toward her. "The tree looks great, sweetie." Randy looked back at me and said, "Ava, this is Hope."

I wanted to blurt out, "I think I'm your cousin," but I refrained.

"Hi, Hope. Nice to meet you." She pointed to the nerdy, but adorable, guy. "That's my friend, Noah."

"Hello," I said, nervously picking at the hem of my shirt as I felt his gaze lock onto mine. His jet-black hair framed a face that radiated warmth, while his tan skin and deep brown eyes sent a tingle down my spine. I couldn't help but feel exposed under his intense stare.

"You kids are about the same age," Randy said as he looked at Ava and Noah. "Hope's new in town. Maybe you could show her around?"

"Sure, can do," Ava said.

Noah nodded; his gaze glued to mine as a smile tugged at the corners of his mouth.

Randy put his hand on Noah's shoulder. "Noah's like family. He and Ava have been best friends since they were in diapers."

Noah's face turned beet red.

I meticulously surveyed my surroundings. My gaze landed on a bookshelf that stretched from one wall to another. A framed photograph of a man and a woman was nestled among the shelves. I couldn't believe what I was seeing. I blinked a few times. I would almost swear I was staring at myself in the photo, but my sandy-blonde hair was brown.

Holding the frame in my hand inches from my nose, I squinted as my eyes scoured every inch of the photo. Pausing to look up, I locked eyes with Randy. "Who's this woman?"

"Why don't we all sit down," Randy said and motioned everyone toward the sunroom. "Ava, you, too. Come sit."

Noah hesitated but went back to decorating the tree.

My face tightened as I looked at the picture again. "Who is this?" I demanded.

Confused, Ava looked at Renee.

"Please sit. I'll explain everything," Randy said.

Clutching the photograph, I followed Randy into the sunroom and sat on the wicker couch. Ava and Renee shuffled in behind me.

I took a deep breath, hoping the additional oxygen would keep me from passing out.

"The woman in the photograph is my sister, and the man with her is her husband, Josh Miller, who is the owner of this house."

My eyes began to fill with tears. "I thought I was looking at myself."

"Her name was Elizabeth Levine, and she was your mother. I believe you're our niece."

Ava noisily gulped. She grabbed Renee's hand, who had begun to cry.

"Janie?" Renee said, her voice breaking.

I choked back the tears and bit my lip. "No. My name is Hope Miller. I don't know any Janie," I lied. *That was stupid.* This reunion was overwhelming, and I didn't know what else to do.

"You came here looking for the owner of this house, right?" Randy moved to sit next to me and looked at the picture. He pointed to Josh. "Why are you looking for him?"

"I should go." I pushed the warm metal frame into his hand. Seeing a picture of my mom sent me into emotional overdrive. She was beautiful, so young and vibrant.

"Wait, Hope. Please don't go," Randy pleaded. "I'm your uncle. Your mother was my sister. This is your Aunt Renee and your cousin Ava." He repeated the family tree again as though I didn't believe him the first time.

I bolted toward the front door.

Randy chased after me. "I know this must be a lot to take in, but I'm certain you're my niece. You look just like your mother."

I shouted with my hand on the doorknob, "I'm sorry. I'm not who you think I am. I need to go." I pulled open the door and padded toward my car. *Two, three, five, seven.* Counting primes in my head always helped calm me down. I jumped into the driver's seat and backed out of the driveway like the house was on fire.

Randy

Ava and Renee arrived at the front door with Hope's dog in tow.

Feeling defeated, I shrugged and said, "She left."

"Are you sure that was Janie, Dad?" Ava asked, her eyes wide with excitement.

"I mean as sure as I can be without a DNA test. Renee, you saw her. What do you think?"

Renee nodded. "It most definitely was her."

Ava spun around and smiled. "If she's my cousin, that'll be so freaking cool." Her orange-red hair bobbed up and down as she flitted down the hallway. "I never thought I'd get to meet her."

I placed my hand on her shoulder. "Ava, honey. Calm down. We don't know for sure if that girl is your cousin. And even she is, she'll need time to process."

Renee bent down to pet the dog, who gleefully wagged her tail. "What do we do with the dog?"

"Let's keep her. Maybe Hope will come back for her," I said.

We ordered pizza for lunch and spent the afternoon decorating the house. Ava and Noah put every ornament on the massive tree, all two hundred and fifty. Each was topped with a matching gold bow.

With his hands on his hips, Noah said, "This is quite the tree." A look of admiration filled his face. "I hate to decorate and run, but I need to get to my shift at the bookstore."

"Thanks for the help today," Renee said.

Ava walked Noah out.

Renee and I decorated the garland on the fireplace mantle, sunroom doorway, dining room chandelier, and entry doorway. We took special care to cover each with a strand of lights, red and gold poinsettias, and gold pinecones. DD followed us through each room. She stood by, intent and quiet, watching us work.

"I think the dog is watching us," Renee said.

DD groaned and tilted her head to the side.

"Do you know we're talking about you?" Renee softened her voice and rubbed her nose against the dog's.

"She does seem to be a good dog," I said.

DD laid down, crossed her paws, and rested her head on her legs. She watched us while we finished putting up the last strand of garland. We packed up and were about to lock the front door when the old gray Land Rover came racing into the driveway.

An arm shot out the window and waved. "I left the dog," Hope bellowed from inside the vehicle.

I casually walked toward the car. "I didn't mean to overwhelm you earlier."

"You didn't. Well, maybe I am a little overwhelmed."

DD stood in the doorway of the house. She turned in circles on the porch and barked. "DD. Stop barking," Hope shouted.

Renee sat on the porch swing, and DD rested her head on her knee.

"DD, come. It's time to go," Hope shouted again.

"I don't think DD's ready to leave," I said.

Hope put the car in park but left the engine running. As she approached the front porch, she called for DD. "Defiant as ever." She rolled her eyes. DD didn't budge.

Hoped shifted her weight. "I guess she wants to stay with you. She's not my dog, anyway. Do what you want with her," Hope said. "Bye, DD. I'm leaving."

The dog ran to the edge of the porch as Hope sauntered away. She began to bark wildly. Hope turned around. Tapping her toe, she snapped, "What? What do you want?"

DD sat back on her hind legs. Her tongue hung out the side of her mouth as she panted.

"I think she wants you to stay," I said. "Please stay? Talk to us."

Hope looked down at the ground and then back up at me. "The woman in the picture was my mom? You're her brother?"

"I'm as sure as the Southport sunsets."

FIVE

Hope

I don't know why I decided to come back for the damn dog. I didn't understand the emotions that were swirling around in my stomach. Logic was my ally, a realm that I could comprehend and rely on. The intense emotions from the family reunion had me twisted up inside. Waves of fear mixed with curiosity disabled my logic meter. My heart was like a robot on the fritz, my head spinning as I tried to process countless emotions. On the one hand, this could be my mother's brother and his family, the family I longed to meet and get to know for most of my life. On the other hand, it could be a creeper who wanted to take advantage of me or, more likely, my father.

I was raised to trust the people on my ranch and no one else. Josh Miller and the rest of my Southport family were the only exceptions to this rule. However, I hadn't met any of them. Right now, instinct was the only tool I had to determine the truth. What are the chances that my uncle and his family would be at the house with the red roof at the exact moment I showed up?

My instincts told me to run and head back to Ismay, Montana. Every cell in my body screamed for me to go home and give up my search. But I had left the damn dog, and I had to go back for her.

Who was I kidding? I came back because I was curious. I came back because I wanted to know more. I drove across the country to finally meet anyone who had a connection to my mother. I came back to be closer to my mother. Now, standing in front of a man who claims to be her brother, I can't run.

Renee's and Ava's eyes radiated with innocence and heartache. They wanted me to be Janie as badly as I wanted them to be my aunt and cousin. I stood leaning against my car and maintained a safe distance. "How do I know you're telling me the truth?"

Randy slowly approached me and said, "We're telling you the truth. What you decide to believe is up to you."

I pushed around some loose pebbles in the driveway as I considered what to say next. "My father told me I lived in a house with a red roof. He said I lived here with my mother and Josh. I came to find Josh. Except he isn't here, and you could be anyone."

Renee and Ava walked toward me as Renee said, "We aren't anyone. We're your family. We have waited years for this day." A tear trickled from the corner of her eye.

Randy's voice quivered as he said, "I'm your mother's brother. I've grieved for Lizzie every day since she died. You look just like her."

I didn't know what to say. I had envisioned this moment a thousand times, and now my tongue was tied in knots.

Renee looked past me into my car. "What's that hanging from your rearview mirror?"

I turned to see what she was looking at. "It's a Saint Christopher medal. Why?"

Renee held out her hand. "Can I see it?"

I thought the request was odd, but I obliged. I climbed inside the car and pulled the chain off the mirror. Dangling from my fingertips, Renee took the medal and rubbed her thumb across the top. Tears spilled down her cheeks. She looked up and said, "I gave this to you the day you and Gray left Southport."

I furrowed my brow and looked at her. Studying her face, I couldn't find anything but genuine joy in her eyes. My father told me my Aunt Renee had given me the medal. When he gave me the Land Rover, he insisted I hang it from the rearview mirror to keep me safe. A tidal wave of emotions crashed over me, and once again, I thought I might short-circuit. My knees weakened, my heart beat rapidly, and my eyes welled up. I fought hard to choke back my emotions but failed. Tears streaked down my cheeks as Randy and Renee wrapped their arms around me, followed by Ava.

Unable to breathe and uncomfortable with the hugging, I stepped back and wiped my cheeks. DD trotted from the porch and sat beside me. Her tail wagged furiously and brushed the ground. She lifted her paw and nudged my leg. I looked down. "What, dog? What do you want?"

She groaned, then lay down, her puppy dog eyes looking up at me.

"You're my Uncle Randy," I said as I looked toward him. "My actual uncle? And you're my aunt and my cousin. My family?" I was excited but needed time to process what I was learning.

Beaming, Randy said, "We sure are." He rocked back and forth. "We'd love to have you for dinner sometime soon. We have a Friends of Southport meeting, but we can get together tomorrow night."

I put my hands in my pocket and rocked back on my heels. My eyes were focused on the tips of my shiny white tennis shoes. "Are you sure?"

"Of course, we're sure," Randy and Renee said simultaneously.

SIX

Randy

His black hair was shaggy and matted, and the hair on his face was even worse. Crumbs of food or perhaps crusted snot were stuck inside his beard, which hung down to his chest. "Good gracious, man. You look like garbage," I said.

"I didn't ask you to come here. And I certainly didn't ask for your opinion," Josh snapped.

"Well, too bad. Maybe you need to hear that you look like shit. You've made an art form of avoiding everyone, and you've turned into an epic piece of shit. Despite all that, I thought you'd like to know Janie's come home."

A glimmer of joy appeared in his gray eyes, which were once a vivid blue. Just as fast as the glimmer appeared, it disappeared. "Get the hell off my dock," Josh barked, smashing his fist against the railing. "Is it fun for you to torment me? I spent ten years trying to find the bitch who killed your sister and another ten trying to find Janie. You're sick, man."

My heart ached, and I pitied him. My sister's death had turned his heart to stone. He had not been able to move on. For twenty years, the loss of my sister and Janie had fueled anger inside of him as deep and wide as the Grand Canyon. He's been a prisoner of the past, driven by revenge and hate, unable to move on. The hardness on his face, the lines etched into his forehead, and the dark circles under his eyes told the story.

I gently placed my hand on his shoulder and spoke softly. "Bro, you're family, whether you want to acknowledge that or not. I'd never make something like that up. Janie *is* home. She's coming to dinner tomorrow. I thought maybe you'd like to join us."

Josh ran his hand through his matted hair as if he had suddenly recognized what a mess he was. He smoothed his hands down the tattered gray T-shirt he wore and looked down at his filthy attire.

I removed my hand from his shoulder and said, "Gray named her Hope Miller."

Josh stumbled backward into the railing at the sound of his last name. A single tear spilled from the corner of his eye and glistened in the sunlight. "You need to go," Josh said, waving his arm at me. "I don't want you here. I don't want anyone here. I want to be left alone."

"Okay, Bro, I'll go." I turned to leave and paused. "She looks just like Lizzie. She's beautiful."

I got halfway down the dock when Josh hollered, "Randy, wait." He held up his right hand with his pointer finger in the air as he ran down the dock and climbed into his boat. When he returned, he was holding a notebook in his hand. "Give this to Janie. It was her mother's. Lizzie would want her to have it."

"I suppose you won't be joining us for dinner, then?" I took the book and tucked it under my arm.

"No. She doesn't want to see me. What am I to her?" He put his hands on the railing and looked out at the water. "I'm just the guy her mother married who almost became her dad, but never really got the chance."

Before I could respond, he shook his head and walked away.

Hope

My breath quickened as I approached the porch, and I considered running back toward the car. DD trotted along behind me. I stood at the front door, fidgeting with the hem of my sweatshirt as I contemplated knocking. DD looked up at me, her puppy dog eyes glowing in the porch light. "I'm going. I'm going. I need a minute." She pawed at my thigh. I sighed and dropped my head. I couldn't knock. I couldn't lift my arm and make my hand knock on the slick wooden door. Just as I turned to leave, DD began to jump and bark. Light poured onto the porch as the front door swung open, and Randy stood there smiling with his eyes and mouth.

"Janie, we're so glad you're here."

My muscles tightened. "Please, call me Hope," I said, barely meeting his eyes with mine.

"All right, Hope. We're so glad you're here. Come in." He smiled as he said the words, but his eyes filled with sadness.

I took a small step into the house. It appeared newly renovated and freshly cleaned, and the scent of lemon lingered in the air. Scanning the room, my gaze fell upon a back door in the kitchen and a small window above the sink, an instinct my father had engrained in me.

Always be sharp, Hope. Never let your guard down. Have a plan before you need one; be prepared for anything.

With my father's words ringing in my head, I missed the comfort of my ranch in Montana, my haven. Over the years, I encased my heart in cement. Logic was my best friend. My father said emotions lead to distraction, and I could never afford to be distracted.

As I stood in the living room of my aunt and uncle's house, a wide range of emotions swirled through me like a tornado, and suddenly, I felt sick to my stomach. My knees became weary, and I stumbled into the back of the couch. The soft, brown leather was cold in the palm of my hand, and I looked at the strangers before me.

My family.

I could see the love mixed with pain in their eyes, and I...well, I was nothing short of confused. I didn't understand how to unpack my feelings.

DD broke the awkward silence as she jumped, performed circles in mid-air, and then rubbed her body against Randy's leg.

Ava said, "Aww. Come here, puppy," as she patted her legs and beckoned for the dog to come to her.

"I'm sorry. She kind of does what she wants. She doesn't always listen to me."

Ava ran her fingers along the top of DD's head. "She's sweet. She just wanted some love and attention." Her voice was childlike and high-pitched.

Beep. Beep. Beep.

"That's dinner," Renee said.

Randy moved quickly to the stove. "I'll get it."

Renee put her hands on my shoulders. "I'm sure this is overwhelming. We don't have any expectations. We're just glad you're here." She smiled, and I let out a puff of air. I think I held my breath from the moment I arrived. "We loved your mother, and we've prayed every day that you'd return to us. We are so glad you're here."

"I'm glad to meet you, too. My father told me about you."

"He did?" Randy asked as he set the lasagna onto the kitchen table.

"Yes. He talked about you. He told me about Helen and Josh, too, and the bookstore. My father loved this place. I could see it in his eyes when he spoke. When I was a little girl, he'd sit by my bed and tell me stories of Southport. That's what he called it."

Renee's eyes glistened as they filled to the brim with tears. She smoothed her shirt down with her hands. "Who's hungry?"

DD barked, and laughter filled the room, creating a sense of calm.

Ava and I sat across from Randy and Renee. The scent of basil and oregano wafted through the house, which caused my mouth to salivate. "It smells delicious," I said.

Randy rubbed his belly. "You know I'm ready. Let's eat." He scooped a heaping mound of lasagna onto his plate.

I scanned the room again, but this time, I saw the love that existed there. Photos of the three of them on the beach, at a parade, at Disney World. Countless memories were captured behind glass frames like time portals to the past. I smiled and accidentally let out a small chuckle.

"What's funny?" Randy said.

My cheeks turned red from embarrassment.

"What?" he said again.

I played with the food on my plate, pushing meat crumbs into a pile. "Your hair," I said. "My father always described you with hair. It's why I wasn't sure I believed you earlier today." I shoved a forkful of lasagna in my mouth to shut myself up. I pointed to a picture on the wall. "But you did have hair. Auburn and wavy, just like my father described it."

Renee roared with laughter so hard she started to cry. "He did have hair. You're correct. That was a long time ago."

Randy contorted his lips and rolled his eyes upward as he rubbed his bald head. "What? You don't like my bald head."

We all laughed again.

After dinner, we walked through town and got some ice cream. I'm not sure what I was so nervous about. Spending time with them was easy, and getting to know them was nice. Ava was quiet but kind. I'm sure this was somewhat overwhelming for her, too.

"Do you plan to stay?" Renee asked.

"I think so. My father will probably want me to come home, but I think I'd like to stay for a while. I drove across the country, so I might as well settle in for a bit."

"Where are you staying?" Randy said.

"I'm not sure yet. I planned to shop around for a place tomorrow."

"Tomorrow? Where have you been sleeping?" Renee gasped.

"I've been sleeping in the car with DD. It's quite comfortable with the seat fully reclined."

Renee shook her head. "Oh no, ma'am. Absolutely not. You'll stay here tonight," she said sternly.

"Thank you, but I'm fine, really. I don't want to stay here." I wished I could rephrase my words when I saw the hurt appear in their eyes. I'm too direct for my own good sometimes. That's what my father says.

Randy opened his mouth to speak, but Renee gently touched his forearm. "You always have a place here with us. We have an apartment in the back. We rebuilt it years ago and recently renovated it when we redid the house. It's yours if you want it, rent-free."

"Thank you. It's nice of you to offer. DD and I plan to check out a few places tomorrow. I'll keep you posted."

DD stood next to Renee, her tail wagging rhythmically, thumping against the side of Renee's leg.

"I should go. I'm sure DD needs to go outside, and I have a long day ahead of me tomorrow." Randy stepped toward me and wrapped his arms around me. I froze like a statue with my arms by my side. "Thanks for dinner," I muttered.

Renee swooped in for a hug. *Okay, we're doing this, I guess. We're all getting hugs.* I did my best not to tense up, but it wasn't easy. Ava jumped in on the hugs, too. I did my best to act natural.

I opened the door to leave.

"Wait," Randy said. "I'll be right back. Don't go." He disappeared into the office.

I stared silently in the doorway and rocked back on my heels. Randy returned with a notebook in his hand. "Josh gave me this to give to you. He said it was your mother's, and she'd want you to have it."

My words caught in my throat, and my chest tightened. *Was he holding something of my mother's?* Endless possibilities raced through my mind as I considered what I might find inside.

SEVEN

Hope

The morning was mostly a bust. DD and I visited three different rental properties. First, we checked out a room for rent inside the home of a lovely elderly couple, which I considered, but there wouldn't be much privacy. We visited a cute and promising tiny house, but DD peed in the corner, so we fled the scene as fast as possible. Lastly, a condo was available just outside of town in a new high-rise complex. The rent was pricey, and the only place available was on the seventeenth floor. The condo was spacious and beautiful, but not ideal for DD, who had apparently become my permanent pet.

I snagged a parking spot along the water's edge when we drove back into town. DD jumped out of the open window and trotted to my side of the car. "I need to get you a collar and a leash," I whispered as I patted her on the top of the head. She let out a playful yap and swiped her paw across her nose. “Stay close and don’t get crazy.”

I nodded to the man leaning on the black SUV beside mine and called for DD to follow me.

We walked along Moore Street. Many of the shop owners were decorating their store windows. I had never seen anything like it; each window was more extravagant than the next. Animated Christmas carolers, garlands with lights, and enormous glass ornaments adorned the storefronts. I smiled and waved to the workers as they continued their decorative festivities.

Southport was nothing like I imagined. I didn’t quite grasp the charm the town possessed from my father’s stories. Watching the street spin into Christmas before my eyes was reminiscent of a Hallmark movie I enjoyed watching with Louisa, the gardener on the ranch. She was a short, stocky woman with the greenest thumb on the planet. She could bring a dead tree back to life.

DD stayed by my side as we crossed the street to the general store. A bright pink sign hung from the door. The sign read:

Friends of Southport

Meeting: Thursday, November 17th

Time: 7:00 PM

Place: Bayview Books

Led by Helen Loughlin, President of the Historical Society

Join Friends of Southport. We are a group of local people who want to save and preserve the history, health, & beauty of our town. If you, too, care about our town, please attend our meeting so you can help keep the charm in our beautiful town of Southport. Don't change Southport. Let Southport change you.

I stared at the poster and wondered if this Helen was *my* Helen, my mom's best friend and the owner of the famous bookstore my father talked so much about. The sound of a woman shrieking jolted me away from my thoughts, and I snapped my head around to see what was causing the commotion. A slender, elderly woman kicked her leg frantically as her arms flailed through the air. Her silky-smooth silver hair was slicked back into a low bun. The woman used the perfect amount of gel to create a permanent wet look that accentuated her white highlights as they shimmered in the sunlight.

As the woman spun around, I recognized the large, white and brown spotted doodle dog attached to her pant leg. "DD!" I shouted. "DD, No!" I shouted louder. I ran across the street, shouting for DD to leave the poor woman alone. DD growled and snarled. Her canines were dripping with saliva, and her eyes were filled with rage. Her demeanor scared me.

"I'm so sorry. She's never behaved this way before," I said as I tried to pull DD from the death grip she had on the woman's pants leg. "DD. No." I clapped my hands sternly as I shouted one more time. I swear this damn dog had a mind of her own. Sometimes, she was perfect and sweet, and sometimes, she was a complete lunatic trying to eat old ladies as they passed along the street.

DD finally let the elderly woman go and sat back on her hind legs, but continued to growl. "That dog should be shot," the woman said in a huff. "Your nasty mutt needs to be put down. If you won't do it. I will."

Her skin was smooth and white like porcelain, but her scowl showed her age as wrinkles formed across her forehead. She seemed to have ice flowing through her veins. *No wonder DD wanted to chew off your leg.*

"I'm very sorry, ma'am. Are you okay?"

"I'm fine," she huffed. "Your bitch ruined my seven-hundred-dollar pant leg." She looked me in the eye for the first time, and suddenly, her face softened, and her demeanor completely changed. "No, no. I'm sorry. I'm fine. It's fine. I overreacted," she said, brushing off her sweater.

That was a random change of heart.

"I'll be sure to keep her on a leash. Thank you for being so kind about this." I snapped my fingers at DD, who still growled at the woman. "Have a good day," I said as I turned to leave and caught sight of a man standing against the side of the building. He wore a black ball cap pulled down low on his forehead, jeans, and a gray sweatshirt. I swear I had seen him earlier.

Our eyes locked, and a chill crept over me as he immediately looked away. I couldn't make out his face in the dim light, but a prickle of recognition danced along my skin—he had to be the same guy I'd seen by my car earlier.

Continuing to explore, I grabbed a sandwich, a tasty pastry from this nifty little place called Burney's, water, and a pup cup from the ice cream place for DD. The Land Rover door creaked as I opened it. DD hopped right in and curled up in a ball, resting her head on the console between our seats.

I climbed into my seat and let out a sigh. "What a day, huh, girl?"

DD also let out a big squeal as she yawned and looked up at me with her big, brown eyes. "Promise me you won't eat anymore old ladies?" DD sat up and started to growl again. "Whoa. Down, girl. It's okay." I rubbed her chest and patted my hand on the center console, beckoning her to lie back down.

I leaned back against the headrest and closed my eyes. Drawing a long breath, I exhaled slowly and began to relax. I could hear DD rustling around, and I opened one eye to see what she was doing. Her front paws were down on the floorboard, and her tail wagged frantically back and forth. She sprang up with the red notebook in her teeth. She gently set it on the center console and lay back down.

Terrified, I looked down and stared at my mother's notebook. Once more, a wave of emotions surged through me, leaving me bewildered. My leg jittered restlessly as my throat tightened, my heart raced faster, and my palms became clammy. I was inundated with a torrent of feelings and unable to decipher them all at once. DD placed her paw onto the notebook and gently nudged it toward me.

I took another deep breath and opened the cover. I traced the letters on the page with my index finger and imagined my mother sitting quietly, writing this very message. My skin burned as a tear slid down my cheek. My heart skipped a beat as I read the words on the page before me.

Dear Janie Bug,

Today is the day we met. I saw your most perfect and beautiful face for the first time. I remember staring at you in an effort to permanently etch every inch of you into my mind. My heart swelled with so much love the instant I laid eyes on you. I thought my heart might burst inside my chest. I need you to know that I did not give you up by choice. You were taken from me against my will. I loved you from the second I heard your heart beating on the ultrasound monitor. I'm sorry that this evil was brought into our lives, but I love you, Janie Bug, and I always will. I want to be the best mom I can be for you. I've started this journal to share stories and inspirational thoughts with you, and someday, when the time is right, I'll share them with you.

Mom's WOW – Words Of Wisdom

I hope that you will learn to have faith. Faith is an essential part of living. Martin Luther King Jr. said it best: "Faith is taking the first step, even when you don't see the whole staircase."

Life will not always be kind to you, Janie Bug, but you must have faith. Faith that things will work out exactly as they are intended. Even when you don't understand why life has treated you in a certain way, you have faith that you are exactly where you are supposed to be at that moment. Have faith in yourself and your family. Family is important, Janie Bug. Be there for your family and lean on them when you need help.

When I woke up in the hospital, and they told me that I had lost you, my world collapsed. I didn't want to take another breath. My heart hurt too much. But I took that first step and kept taking one step at a time every day after knowing that somehow it would all work out exactly how God had intended, and today, I got to hold you, my precious Angel. Against all odds, we found our way back to each other.

Always remember to have faith. I love you big.

Love, Mom

As my tears soaked the pages, the ink started to run, and my trembling hands made the book shudder. Life in Montana had always been uncomplicated. For twenty years, logic served as a guiding beacon, illuminating my path. However, after spending three days in Southport, I found myself grappling with an array of emotions that were entirely new. One part of me wanted to continue reading, while the other longed for the solace of my Montana home. For a moment, I wished to forget this chapter of my life.

My mother, Lizzie Levine Miller, kept a diary or journal meant for me, and here I am in the town she adored, clutching her words in my hand, engulfed by grief and sorrow. Anger settled deep within me, and I became consumed by rage. Someone took my mother away, leaving me to spend most of my life yearning to make her proud, longing to hold her hand, hear her voice, or embrace her.

But I can't.

A very sick and cruel individual robbed me of a life with my mother.

I slammed the book shut and tossed it on the dashboard. My skin felt itchy. I sighed deeply, started the car, and headed to Uncle Randy's house. *Uncle. That's so weird.* I decided I needed a decent place to sleep.

My car wasn't going to cut it any longer.

EIGHT

Montana - Past

Gray

I lay in the grass. My eyes squinted as the sun's rays beat down on my face. Three hundred and sixty-five days had passed since Lizzie was taken from us, and I was left to raise our precious daughter. *I'm a horrible person. How can I ever provide for Janie the way she deserves to be cared for?* Janie deserved to be loved unconditionally. I loved her with all my heart, but I wasn't the greatest example of how to love. *Dear God, I know I don't pray to you often, if ever. But could you please help me not fuck this up?*

Ismay, Montana, had a total population of seventeen people, and eleven of the residents were my employees who lived on the ranch. Four hundred acres of prairies and rolling hills, with streams and a pond in the front yard. *No trespassing* signs hung from the barbed wire fence that surrounded the entire property, and all four hundred acres were under constant video surveillance. The Kaffi Ranch was a fortress. Lizzie loved coffee, and wanting to feel connected to her, I selected the name in her honor. Kaffi is Icelandic for coffee. I liked the Iceland version of the word better.

I climbed onto a hay bale in the farthest corner of the ranch and hung my head. My heart ached with a void so large I thought it might split me in half. Janie looked more like Lizzie every day. Today was the three hundred and sixty-fifth day we had spent at Kaffi Ranch. A mouse scurried past my feet into the trees. My mind wandered to thoughts of Lizzie. I owed her everything. She pulled me from the darkness to the light and showed me how to be part of a family. She taught me how to love another human being and how to let others love me. Most importantly, she gave me Janie. I swiped my foot along the grass and sighed. We survived the last year, but just barely.

Like a movie, I played a few scenes in my mind. Janie sat on the couch in the library with her arms crossed and a frown on her face.

Dr. Abbott's face filled the computer screen. "Hope, do you know why I'd like to talk to you today?" His wire-rimmed glasses sat on the tip of his nose. Janie huffed and looked away. "Can you tell me about your ranch?" He tried another question.

Janie lay down and played with the stitching on the pillow. "Dr. Abbott, maybe we should try again another day. She isn't ready," I said, sitting on the floor next to the couch. I rubbed Janie's head, hoping she'd look at me. Instead, she buried her head in the crease of the couch.

Dr. Abbot smoothed his gray hair that combed over his balding head. "That's fine. Let's try again next week."

I opened the door and called for Keith.

Keith helped orchestrate the secure Zoom call with Dr. Abbott. Keith was part of the ranch security detail and a wizard with computers, the Internet, and technology. I didn't know most of what he'd done in his life before the ranch, and I didn't want to know, but on the Kaffi Ranch, he ensured we had secure wireless Internet connections.

My eyes moistened as I recalled the countless times I logged onto the Zoom sessions with Dr. Abbott. Janie's behavior grew increasingly worse. I clutched my chest as I remembered the session where Janie flung herself to the floor. She kicked her legs and flailed her arms as she screamed and cried. Sliding off the hay bale to the ground, the hurt welled inside me as I relived the moment. *Damn it!*

Eventually, I did what any respectable father would and tricked her. Memories continued to flood into focus.

"Keith, can you set up a camera in the kitchen that will stream to Dr. Abbott's computer?"

Keith glanced at me sideways. "Of course I can, sir."

"Great."

Dr. Abbott had sent me a list of questions, which I shared with Mr. Geoffrey, our resident chef. Janie was in the library, hiding in the corner. She was an intelligent girl. She was aware it was time for her session, but as usual, she didn't want to participate.

"Hope. Where are you?" I sang, pretending I didn't know where she was. She scooted a little further back into the corner. I wandered around the room, opening drawers and cabinets. I peeked behind books on the bookshelf and looked out the window. Standing in the center of the room, I stood with my hands on my hips and said, "Where could Hope be?"

Like a flash of lightning, I turned and let out a roar as I grabbed Janie's sides. She screamed and began to giggle. I scooped her into my arms and kissed her cheeks. "How about we make some ice cream?"

Her smile widened as she nodded. She wrapped her arms around my neck, and I thought my heart might explode.

My heart filled with joy as I sat slumped against the hay bale. Week after week, Janie made ice cream with Mr. Geoffrey. He and I followed Dr. Abbott's instructions, gently probing and asking questions while we mixed the heavy cream. Every morning and night, I read to Hope and told her stories of Southport. Dr. Abbott said it was essential to help her feel safe and loved. He said Janie's exposure to the death of her mother caused trauma that could impair her social-emotional development. I would do anything to take the pain away from my little girl.

A bird squawked as it flew into my vision, and a knee slammed into my gut. "Ugh," I scowled.

"Father. Did you see the birdie?"

A smile spread across my face—a complete sentence with the slightest hint of expression in her tone.

"Father, why are your eyes wet? You okay?" She placed her little hand on my cheek.

I sat up and wrapped her in my arms. "Yes, Hope. Everything's wonderful."

NINE

Montana – Past

Hope

Dr. Eleanor Fleen was firmly planted in her chair at the desk in the center of our mansion's library on Kaffi Ranch. My father was relentless about my education and insisted I learn every day. My education meant several hours spent with Dr. Fleen, who taught me pointless lessons from pointless textbooks that some random person claimed were of significant importance.

Her large, stubby frame peeked out over the desk. "Hope, you're my brightest student."

I rolled my eyes. "I'm your only student."

"Yes, but my colleagues say you are learning four grade levels above your age." She pushed her chair out from the desk and thundered toward me. "I will accept only the best from you, Miss Hope. You will rise to my expectations and the expectations of your father."

Dr. Fleen owed a debt to my father. She lived on the ranch with us, and her main job was to teach me everything I needed to know from books. She began to yammer on about cell division. Bored to tears, I stared at the awful flower print on her skirt and the drab tan color of her button-down shirt.

Studying her outfit became a daily game. She wore the same thing most days, and I meticulously scoured the shirt for new stains or faded spots. I often wondered if she had multiple sets of the same clothes or wore the same outfit every day. She spiced things up in winter with a blue cardigan to keep her warm. Today, her light brown hair was tied back in a braid.

"There are three types of cell division: mitosis, meiosis, and binary fission," Dr. Fleen droned on. My eyes wandered to the hand-crafted African Blackwood shelving, which hung from wall to wall and housed hundreds of books. I wanted to read every book on the shelves before I left the ranch someday. Books with stories of faraway places, romance, and family fascinated me. Our library was exquisite. A round window from ceiling to floor covered the back wall, allowing the sunlight to pour in. I appreciated that Dr. Fleen stood with her back to the window so I could stare outside at the rolling hills and beautiful farmland. The property was truly magnificent and peaceful.

Sensing my distraction, Dr. Fleen bellowed, "Pop quiz." She clapped her hands, forcing my focus back to her. She reached for a piece of paper on her desk and slammed it in front of me. "Let's see how much you can remember from our lesson today."

Boring!

I sighed, picked up my pencil, and quickly answered each of the fifteen questions. Five minutes later, I handed my quiz to Dr. Fleen. "Done."

She reviewed my answers and shook her head. "I don't know how you do it. Everything is correct." Placing my hands on the desk, I interlaced my fingers and waited patiently. "You can pick a book." She pointed to the fiction section of the bookshelf.

As a reward for good grades, Dr. Fleen would let me select a book of my choosing. I ran my finger along the spines of the books as I scanned in search of the perfect one. I couldn't decide between *Dead Poet's Society* or *The Secret History*, so I snatched both off the shelf.

Dr. Fleen waved her finger in the air. "You know the drill. Only one."

With a loud huff, my shoulders slumped as I considered which book to choose. Finally, I handed her *The Secret History*, flopped onto the oversized brown leather couch, fluffed the pillow for my head, laid back, and started reading.

An hour later, Dr. Fleen said, "That's enough for today, Hope. You're dismissed."

I packed my bag and ran out of the house to the barn to meet up with Gabe.

Gabe was Louisa's son. Louisa was our gardener who cultivated the crops on the ranch. She was like a nature whisperer when it came to caring for plants. What plants needed to grow where and at what time of year? You asked Louisa. She possessed ten green fingers, not just a green thumb. My favorite ranch lessons were the practical ones that taught me real-life skills.

I enjoyed my lessons in the garden with Louisa because they had a purpose. Wanting to learn everything I could from her, I spent three hours every Monday and Thursday helping her plant, pick, weed, and fertilize. Of course, Louisa also had me help her cultivate the compost, which was my least favorite part of gardening, but I appreciated its importance.

Gabe looked just like Louisa. His tan skin was a soft brown that accented his dark brown eyes and hair. I especially liked the leather cowboy hat his father gave him when he became a teenager. Two years older than me, Gabe was the closest I had to a friend my age. He spent most of his time helping his dad, Dante, a full-fledged cowboy. Gabe was his apprentice and spent most of his time cleaning the barn and stables and caring for the horses.

My heart raced as I approached the barn. I slid the large barn door open and shut it softly behind me. Inside the barn, the ground was covered in fresh hay. A glimmer of light in the corner drew my attention to a pile of hay nestled against the wall. Draped across the pile was a gray and white checkered blanket.

Gabe looked as proud as a peacock. "You brought a blanket," I said with a smile.

"I sneaked it from my room last night and hid it in here. After I cleaned out the barn today, I set this up for you." He patted the ground between his legs. "Come and sit. Read to me."

I scootched into him and relaxed against his chest. He rested his chin on my head. I cracked open the book and began to read it out loud.

Gabe couldn't read. He wasn't educated, but I cherished the moments spent reading to him in the barn, even though we technically weren't supposed to be alone together. Reading to Gabe in the barn motivated me to pass Dr. Fleen's stupid tests so I could devour more books from my father's bookshelves.

TEN

Hope

Parked on the street a few houses down from Uncle Randy's house, I sat in the driver's seat of the Land Rover while I worked up the courage to knock on his door. DD lounged in the passenger side, half asleep. I observed my family from a distance. Uncle Randy carried trash through the garage. He tied the bag purposefully before tossing it into a large bin.

Dressed in running pants and sneakers, Aunt Renee shouted for Ava to fill the bird feeders. She kissed Uncle Randy on the cheek before departing for a walk. Ava emerged with three bags of different birdseed. Uncle Randy and Ava worked together to clean out and fill the feeders. I was fascinated by their family dynamic.

Clickity Clop, clickity clop. Clip clop. Clip clop.

Distracted by the noise, my attention was drawn back to the street. A gorgeous Clydesdale horse pulled a sleigh-like carriage.

The coachman was an older man dressed as the Grinch in a Santa suit, with a younger man sitting by his side.

"Ho, ho, ho," the older man called from the passing carriage. I quickly exited my vehicle and flagged down the man. DD sprinted past me and jumped into the back of the carriage. The driver slowed to a stop in front of Uncle Randy's house.

"That's my dog. She's gentle, but excited." I tapped DD's paw as it rested on the edge of the carriage. "I'm Hope."

"I'm the Grinch," the old man said with a laugh. "Just kidding. The name's Joe and this here's my sidekick, Noah."

The younger man turned and smiled, his eyes lingering a second longer than polite. "Nice to see you again, Hope."

He remembered my name. I swooned. *Get it together.*

Pointing to the horse, I said, "May I?"

Joe nodded.

I approached the horse slowly from the front and whispered, "Good boy. Good boy." I patted his shoulder. "I have several horses back home."

Joe said, "Angus here's fifteen years old."

"He's a majestic boy," I said, brushing my hand along the horse's neck, aware of Noah's eyes on me. "Beautiful and well taken care of." I glanced over at Joe and Noah. "He appears to have a touch of arthritis in his forelimb. Our vet back home taught me to make this incredible healing ointment. Would you like me to make some for you?"

Joe nodded. "Thank you. I'll try it. Why not?"

Noah's gaze moved from the horse back to me, his expression amused. "You know your horses, huh?"

I nodded, feeling my cheeks warm under his attention.

Noah scratched his finger along the edge of the carriage. Never looking up, he said, "Joe's teaching me. I help him care for Angus."

Just then, Uncle Randy stepped outside, a proud smile on his face. "Hey Joe, this is my niece, Hope."

Joe chuckled. "We've met. She's going to help Angus here with his arthritis."

Clearly impressed, Uncle Randy raised an eyebrow. "I didn't realize we had a horse whisperer in the family."

Noah shot me a playful look, his eyes twinkling. "See, I wasn't the only one."

I hesitated. Rubbing my arm, I said, "I was sort of..." My voice trailed off as I wiped my forehead, feeling the heat rise in my cheeks. "You know, observing you guys."

He squinted, a slight smile tugging at the corner of his mouth. "Observing us?"

Biting the inside of my lip, I shifted from foot to foot. *Shit. Shit. Shit. Just spit it out.* I looked at Uncle Randy and said, "I wanted to accept your offer to stay in the apartment out back. If it's still available." Rubbing my hands together, I rocked back onto my heels. "I didn't know how to ask. I sat in my car and observed while I worked up the courage. It's what I do." I shrugged.

Uncle Randy tilted his head, blew out a quick breath, and said, "The apartment's yours. Do you want to stay for dinner?"

That was easy.

I blinked. "Umm, I'd love to. I'd love to stay for dinner." I cleared my throat. "Thank you."

ELEVEN

Hope

A harsh, noisy rattling drowned out the sound of my iPod. DD and I were snuggled in bed and my thoughts drifted back to life in Montana. My father never allowed me to have a cell phone. He said I could be tracked through one. I had an ancient purple iPod that he had given me instead. It came with pre-approved music already installed and did not connect to the Internet. My father didn't trust me to be on the Internet alone. He'd say, "I know you wouldn't do anything intentionally, but we can't be too careful. We don't want crazy Catalina to find us." Crazy Catalina was the lady who murdered my mother.

As the noisy rattling got louder, I nudged DD with my foot. Staring at her brown and white spots, I found one spot shaped like a lopsided heart. I was getting used to having DD around, although I could have done without her snoring, which sounded like a freight train.

Randy and Renee's backyard apartment had been the perfect dwelling for my temporary home away from home. Melting into the comfy couch with a cozy blanket, I wanted to lounge a bit longer, but I needed to start my day. I pinched myself. *Ouch!* I guess I wasn't dreaming about the last week.

I enjoyed every minute of getting to know my Southport family. Time spent with them felt effortless as if I'd known them my entire life. But when I was alone, all I could think about was how much time I'd lost with them.

I continued to observe their family dynamics and watch them interact with each other. Having both a mother and a father was foreign to me. My childhood consisted of my father and several of his employees. I was fascinated by Randy and Renee's relationship with Ava and how normal it all seemed to them. I valued their gift of family.

When we settled on the ranch, my father refused to date anyone. He said he had given his heart to my mother a long time ago and couldn't bear to give it away again. I also think he couldn't trust anyone enough to let them into our secluded life on the ranch.

Bayview Books was on the corner of Moore and Davis. The building stood two stories tall and was crafted of red brick. What appeared to be a brand-new sign sparkled white in the sunlight with bright blue letters that said `Bayview Books.` Ava said the bookstore was hiring. I loved reading books and figured working with my newfound cousin wouldn't be the worst thing in the world.

I punched in the code that Ava had given me and pulled open the heavy wooden door. A gorgeous, ornate, hand-carved wood staircase graced the entrance and led to the second floor. Beautiful crystal chandeliers hung from the ceiling, giving the space the perfect light. I think my jaw unhinged as I took in the magnificence around me.

Ava squealed. "Hope. You came." Excited, she clapped her hands and hurried toward me. "We don't open for another hour, so you came at the perfect time."

"I always imaged the bookstore differently," I said as I traced the craftmanship on the staircase railing with my fingertips.

"What do you mean?" Ava said.

"Well, for starters, my father described this place as the upstairs floor of the building, not the entire building. Or at least that's what I envisioned."

Ava smiled. "You're not wrong. The store was originally just upstairs, but everyone in town loved this place, and Helen and Drew eventually bought the entire building. They've renovated the space completely. Drew's a retired handyman, capable of the renovation, and my dad helped a ton, too."

My eyes scanned the first floor and took in the store's unique flair and beauty. A beautiful armoire with a glass front drew my attention, and I took note of the exit door. Curious, I pointed. "What's that?"

"Come on. I'll give you the tour," Ava said as she grabbed my arm and pulled me further into the store. There was something special about Bayview Books, but I couldn't find the words to describe its charm.

Behind the steps, the room opened to an ample gathering space with leather couches and chairs adorned with red and green Christmas pillows. Two top tables with wooden chess and checkerboards were scattered throughout the first floor. A small coffee bar labeled Southport Coffee Co stood against the back wall.

"We host several events each week, and the people of Southport love Bayview for so many different reasons," Ava said. "It's kind of become a gathering place."

Her red hair was tied into a ponytail that bounced as she walked. Bookshelves of all different shapes and sizes lined the walls. Somehow, the variety added to the ambiance of the store. "This store has quite the vibe," I said.

"Helen and your mom loved this place. Your mom created the idea of having different events in the store, and Helen continued the tradition." Ava poured coffee into a white mug with the Bayview Books logo etched into the ceramic. "I spent most of my time here when I was growing up. I was devastated when Helen decided to sell the store last year. My purpose drove me to step up and run the store. It's important to our family and Helen."

"Wait, did you say Helen sold the bookstore? This bookstore?" I was surprised to hear this news.

"Yes. The store was getting harder for Helen and Drew to manage. She taught me everything about running the store, managing a business, and customer service. Not just any customer service, but Southport customer service." We stopped in front of the glass front armoire. "I know I'm young, but I wanted the challenge. I really enjoy this place."

I stared at myself in the mirror and scanned the bookstore reflected behind me. Ava pulled a skeleton key from her pocket, unlocked the door, and gently tugged it open. "Helen was enamored with pirates and the history of pirates in Southport. She collected these pirate manuscripts. They are not for sale. Customers have to ask permission to view them. Some are hundreds of years old."

Afraid to touch the antique manuscripts, I admired them with my eyes. "Fascinating," I said.

We continued through the store, and I ran my fingers along the edge of the bookshelves as we walked past. "I never imagined she'd sell the bookstore. My father seemed so sure that she would still be here working."

Ava took a sip of her coffee. Her green eyes showed genuine kindness as they peeked over her mug. "Helen spends most of her time heading up the Historical Society now. She's determined to keep the charm in Southport."

In the corner, a set of shelves housed several pieces of unique and sophisticated woodwork—wooden bookstands with intricate designs carved into the edges. There were wooden holders for wine bottles and glasses and cutting boards made of wood with the words *Southport, NC* burned into them. I admired the work and picked up a business card from the holder sitting on the shelf. The card read Randy's Rustic Woodwork. I turned toward Ava and held up the card.

Ava smiled and said, "Yep. That's my dad's work." She beamed with pride.

We walked back to the staircase and up to the second level. "I wanted to buy the store, but I'm just barely old enough to drink legally." She laughed. "No bank was going to give me a loan. My parents considered investing but feared my desire to run the bookstore would fade, and they'd be stuck dealing with it."

I followed Ava upstairs, which opened to a child's paradise of reading treasures. A pirate ship covered in sea creatures stood tall in one corner, with bean bags for kids to sit and read. There was a loft in the other corner. Kids could climb the ladder and flop onto a bean bag couch with a book. When finished, they could ride the bright yellow slide back down to the ground. I wondered what it would have been like to grow up here. I don't remember my mom, but somehow, I could sense her presence in Bayview Books. My heart grew warm, and goose pimples formed on my arms.

"Helen knew you'd be back someday. She wanted you to have a reading paradise to play. She wanted to build a space that your mom would love. I have the best memories of playing pretend in the pirate ship with Noah. Sometimes I was a pirate maiden and sometimes a princess taken captive." She laughed. "Helen said your mom loved pirate stories."

"Who's your friend?" a deep voice called from around the corner. His faded Star Wars T-shirt and wrinkled khaki shorts might not have screamed fashion trendsetter, but seeing his smile again sent a flutter of butterflies dancing in my stomach. He froze when he caught sight of me, his eyes widening. "Umm..."

His muscles tensed, the fabric of his faded T-shirt stretching tightly over his pectorals, with the Millennium Falcon flying across his chest. A deep blush rose up his neck. "Hope. Hi." He drew his arm back into a half-hearted wave. "I didn't realize it was you."

His jet-black hair with the slightest curls flopped every which way, and his brown eyes seemed innocent and honest. I was intrigued by his adorable yet nerdy personality.

Ava smacked him on the arm. "Noah works here with me." She pointed in my direction. "I guess he works with both of us now." She raised her eyebrow as a smile stretched across her face.

Noah continued to stand like a statue. I smiled.

He blinked, still dazed.

"Jesus, Noah. You act like you've never seen a girl before," Ava snapped. She smacked his arm again as if he were a broken piece of machinery that could be fixed with a good kick.

Noah shook his head. "It's nice to see you again." He fiddled with the edge of the bookshelf, his fingers tracing the spines of the books. "Do you, uh, like to read?"

His gaze darted away for a moment and then back to me, his cheeks flushing with an endearing awkwardness. His dorky, works at a bookstore, can't form a sentence kind of mannerism intrigued me and made my insides flutter.

"You must have a way with words." I laughed. "It's nice to see you again, too." I twisted back and forth, nervous energy coursing through me as I spoke, never breaking eye contact with him.

"He's just shy. He gets nervous around pretty girls," Ava said as she gave him a gentle punch on the shoulder.

My cheeks flushed. The butterflies escaped, and a gush of weird tingles invaded my stomach.

Noah rolled his eyes, let out a small sigh, and crossed his arms. "Thanks for that, Ava," he said, his tone dry. "I'm not that bad, am I?" He shot her a playful glare, but a hint of a smile tugged at the corners of his mouth.

"You two will get used to each other. Hope's staying with us in our backyard apartment. And if she accepts the position, she'll start working at the bookstore, too."

I snapped my head to look at Ava. "Are you offering me the job?"

"Of course I am. You're family, and you need a place to work. I run the store and do all the hiring." She raised up on her toes. "So, I guess you're hired if you want the job."

Noah froze again, with a goofy grin on his face.

I didn't know what to say. I hesitated before I said, "Thank you. Yes."

Ava squealed and wrapped her arms around me in a gigantic hug. I looked at Noah and wrinkled my face in surprise. My arms dangled by my side as Ava swung us back and forth. Noah smiled, his enormous brown eyes shining. He looked quite handsome when he didn't look so nervous.

"Can I bring my dog?"

Noah

"Jesus, Noah." Ava smacked my arm the instant Hope left the bookstore. "Settle down."

I pushed the broom along the hardwood. "What?"

Ava glared at me. "You acted like a little boy who's never seen a pretty girl before."

Standing with my hand around the broom handle, I shrugged. "I did. I don't know why, but I get all nervous and sweaty around her." I started sweeping again. "She fascinates me."

Ava took the broom from my hand and looked into my eyes. "I thought you were just acting like a big dork, but you really like her, don't you?"

"I hardly know her." I shrugged. "But I can't stop thinking about her."

Ava's eyes widened. "You're smitten." She danced down the aisle like a schoolgirl, teasing me along the way.

Ava was my best friend. She's always had my back. Typically, she didn't like my taste in girls. Once, she put a frog in my girlfriend's backpack when we were kids. I was so mad I didn't talk to her for a week. Ava was right. Vanessa was not nice, and she treated me like dirt. There was also a brief time during Ava's junior year in high school when we thought we might like each other. She kissed me, and we both immediately spit profusely, each of us declaring our smooch was like kissing a sibling. I laughed at the memory.

"What are you laughing at?" Ava shouted from across the room.

"Wouldn't you like to know?"

She mumbled, "Whatever."

A new shipment of books had arrived, and I was organizing them on the appropriate shelves. A few customers were sitting on the comfy chairs reading. The store was relatively quiet and uneventful. I poured myself a cup of coffee and wondered when Hope's first day would be at the bookstore. I couldn't wait to see her again.

TWELVE

Hope

DD was sprawled out on the new bed I purchased for her this morning. "Don't you have quite the life?" I said, rubbing behind her ear. "Not too long ago, you were a stray. Now look at ya."

She made the slightest squeaking sound as she lifted her head and yawned. I stared around the room with my hands on my hips and marveled at my new space—my very own place. If only my father could see me now. I managed to drive across the country, find a place to live, and secure a job. I had help from family, but he didn't need to know that. I laughed inwardly.

Looking at my newly purchased cell phone, I considered calling him to tell him I was okay. He was probably freaking out by now. I didn't want to hurt him, but I felt suffocated. I couldn't stay in Montana one more day.

Plopping down onto the couch, I thought about my mom living in this apartment. I missed her. Well, I can't say I missed her, exactly. I missed the idea of her. My father did his best. He ensured I was well-educated and could defend myself against any adversary, but he wasn't a mom. I was robbed of the opportunity to grow up with my mother, a void I wasn't sure my heart would ever wholly heal from.

DD yelped. Her tail wagged as she wandered toward me. She barked playfully, her tail wagging even faster now. She began to jump in circles as she barked. "What on earth has gotten into you?" I tried to figure out what she wanted. "Do you need to go outside?"

She stretched her front paws and arched her back, lifting her butt in the air. She rested her head on the end table next to the couch and nudged my mother's notebook toward me. "You want me to read?" She took off like a shot, racing around the small room until she jumped onto the couch and curled up in a ball by my feet. "Okay, DD. I'll read."

Flipping open my mother's journal, I inhaled deeply and exhaled slowly.

Dear Janie Bug,

Gosh, what I wouldn't give to hear you call me Janie Bug. I don't even know the sound of your voice.

Today, Josh asked me to marry him. In front of our closest friends and family on his gigantic boat, he got down on one knee and asked me to be his wife. I'm not sure how I got so lucky. Of course, I said yes.

You know what else? He asked you if he could be your daddy. You smiled big and bright and reached your arms up to him. My heart has never been so whole. You looked absolutely precious in your beautiful new dress.

I thought I had lost you forever, and I thought I would never love again. Your father broke my heart, and I wasn't sure the pieces would ever fit back together, but you came back to me. It's a miracle that you're still alive and back in my life. I'll cherish this second chance forever and love you with all my heart.

I'll always do everything in my power to keep you safe and protect you. I can't wait to watch you grow into the amazing young woman I know you're going to become.

Mom's WOW – Words Of Wisdom

Elenor Wheeler Wilcox once said, "There is no chance, no destiny, no fate, that can circumvent or hinder or control the firm resolve of a determined soul."

We were both determined souls. Determined to find our way back to each other. Even as a baby, your resolve brought you home. You learned at a very young age that life is harsh.

Life has a way of kicking your ass, but you must get up and keep going. I wish I could protect you from this truth, but I can't. No one can.

Believe in fate. Life has a way of working out, even when we don't understand the road ahead. No matter how tough things seem, a greater purpose will always reveal itself.

I know your determination will be unmatched in everything you do, Janie Bug. The world had better look out.

Love, Mom

I closed the book and clutched it to my chest as if it were my mother. I didn't want to let go. A single tear slid down my cheek as I continued to grip my mother's journal and consider her words. My life was straightforward up to this point. My father protected me from everything in the outside world. He was determined to keep me safe. I never fully understood why, but reading my mother's words, "I'll always do everything in my power to keep you safe and protected," helped me have to understand.

DD flipped her head back, exposing her neck. "Okay, girl. I'll rub." I ran my palm up and down her neck. "DD, Josh asked to be my daddy. My father never told me that. He told me about Josh and how much he loved my mother. He never told me Josh wanted me to be part of my life."

I moved my hand to scratch an itch on my nose, and DD arched her head back even further. "Geez, girl. I had an itch." I laughed.

"My father didn't let a day pass without telling me how much he loved my mother. He said, 'I treated your mother poorly, and that was the biggest mistake and regret of my life. She was an incredible woman.' All these years, I resented Josh. I believed he took my mom away from my father. My father told me that letting my mother go was the hardest thing he ever had to do, but she deserved to be happy." DD flapped her tail and rolled over. "I spent most of my life wondering if my mom would still be alive if she'd chosen my father instead of Josh."

I jumped when a knock at the door startled me. DD began to bark furiously. "Coming," I said. A humongous bouquet stared me in the face when I opened the door. Roses, carnations, lilies, and a few more flowers I didn't recognize were stuffed inside a glass vase.

"Delivery for Hope," said a high-pitched voice. A dark-haired girl with wire-rimmed glasses peeked her head out from behind the bouquet.

"Thank you," I said, taking the vase from the girl. "DD, we got some flowers."

A card, clipped to the blue bow tied around the vase, read, "Welcome to Southport. I'll be watching over you. Much love with a little drawn heart."

The card wasn't signed. I assumed the flowers were from Randy and Renee. I figured I'd thank them later.

THIRTEEN

Hope

Determined to reach the earth, the sun crept through the giant oak tree branches. Montana was beautiful, but I had never seen trees like those in Southport. As DD and I passed each oak tree, I wondered what stories it could tell. The age and beauty of each oak were breathtaking. Branches stretched like a canopy across the road, providing incredible shade. The tree trunks had massive girth with a diameter of at least five feet. I considered the years these majestic oak trees had witnessed.

DD and I turned up the block and headed toward the water. The sun's reflection cast a blinding light along the water's edge. A twinge of sadness filled my chest as we passed the house with the red roof. I briefly imagined what life could have been like if I had grown up in that house with my mother. We continued walking past the restaurants toward the yacht basin. A variety of boats were tied up along the dock. The sun kissed my skin, and I reached my arms overhead to stretch.

Wagging her tail, DD walked ahead along the dock. She found a stranger to entertain her, a scruffy-looking man who I figured was homeless. His clothes were faded and tattered, his hair was shaggy and matted, and I was afraid creatures may have taken up residence inside his beard. DD didn't seem to mind the man as he petted the top of her head.

"I'm sorry. She's friendly, but sometimes, she has a mind of her own," I said.

He looked up. His eyes were pensive, and I could see brief glimpses of profound sadness. A heaviness rested on his soul.

Our eyes locked, causing an awkward pause. Confused, I tilted my head. His eyes narrowed and then widened. He opened his mouth to speak but was interrupted.

"I think Mrs. Millie's boat is ready," said a familiar voice.

I've only known approximately twenty-five people my entire life, including those I've met in Southport. I was confident I recognized this voice.

Beads of sweat shimmered as they slid down his perfectly tanned skin. His pectoral muscles flowed perfectly into his abdomen, which was clad in tie-dye bathing suit shorts. My mouth was still open, and I slammed it shut but could not peel my eyes away. He was a fine specimen; perhaps his body had been created in a lab, an exceptional human, even by most people's standards.

"Oh, sorry, I didn't realize you were with a cust..." The man with the familiar voice froze.

I blinked the sun out of my eyes. *Noah?*

DD barked, drawing my attention.

"She's not a customer," the homeless man snapped. His expression was pained. "You assumed wrong."

Noah raised his hands in surrender. "Okay, Josh. My bad."

I stepped forward and clapped my hands for DD to come. "Noah?" *Jesus, take the wheel. Noah was H-O-T, hot.* I wasn't sure how it was possible, but he was getting cuter every time I saw him.

"Hope?"

The homeless man looked at me and then back at Noah. "You two know each other?"

I furrowed my brow and looked at Noah. "You know this homeless man?"

Noah roared.

I cocked my hip to the side and crossed my arms. My patience in the confusion was wearing thin.

Sensing my frustration, Noah scratched the back of his neck and said, "I'm sorry, Hope. This is Josh Miller, my boss. I help him with the boats on the dock when I'm not at the bookstore." Noah raised his hand. "Oh, and he's not homeless. Well, maybe he's partly homeless. He has a home but lives out here on his boat."

Could this be my mom's husband? He looks like a homeless man. Josh Miller is a common name. Perhaps there are two in Southport?

Josh pressed his hands into the railing on the edge of the dock and looked out toward the water. "Yes. I'm Josh Miller. I was going to introduce myself, but Noah interrupted me."

"Hope's staying with Randy and Renee," Noah said. I caught his eyes traveling up and down my body. Josh caught it, too, and smacked him on the back of the head.

DD trotted by and sat beside me. I patted her head and said, "I'm Hope Miller. Are you the Josh who married Lizzie Levine?"

He turned away and began walking down the dock. DD chased after him. I looked at Noah, who frowned. "Hey," I shouted. "I asked you a question. What's your problem?" *Wow. I sounded just like my father.*

Josh stopped dead in his tracks. "What's my problem? What's mmmyyyyy problem?" He shook his head and waved us off.

I ran toward him, put my hands on his chest, and shoved him. "I can't believe she chose you. You're a bum. You hide out here on your boat and avoid living. You look like garbage." Years of rage welled inside, and I balled my fists and slammed them against his chest. He stood there and let me. He didn't move.

"I loved your mother," Josh said. I gave him one final hit, then crossed my arms and rolled my eyes. I pitied him. He looked homeless, sad, and alone. "I dedicated a decade of my life trying to find your father's batshit crazy wife." He shifted his weight and lowered his head. "I wanted nothing more than to avenge your mother's death, but I couldn't find Catalina. She vanished."

My father's wife? Catalina is my father's wife? My father left out that small, extremely relevant detail. Was my entire life one big lie?

"I failed. I prefer to keep to myself, and I would appreciate it if you'd leave now," Josh said, his voice sharp and clipped.

DD rubbed her body against my leg and whimpered softly.

FOURTEEN

Noah

Dipping my brush into the giant bucket, I said, "You okay, man? That was pretty intense."

Josh massaged his heart. "My chest burns like someone pressed a hot branding iron to my skin. I can almost smell my flesh burning." He inhaled and closed his eyes. He continued as he exhaled. "Every day for twenty years, my heart ached for her mother, Lizzie. I was bitter and angry. Seeing Janie brought on a flood of emotions that I wasn't ready to deal with."

I pressed my lips together. "I can't imagine how difficult this must be, but it's a good thing she's back, right?" I shrugged, not sure what to say. "Oh, and Josh, she prefers to be called Hope."

I wasn't sure he was fully listening to me. He seemed to be staring off into space. "She radiates beauty just like her mother. She has her grit, too. Helen was right. Gray named her Hope, but

I couldn't believe he gave her my last name." He shook his head. "Hope Miller."

His knees weakened and almost gave way when her name rolled off his tongue.

"She is a babe. I get so awkward around her," I admitted, a nervous chuckle escaping as I scratched my arm.

Josh smacked the back of my head again.

"She's not available," he said with a growl.

"Yes, sir. Are ya sure? I'd treat her right." My face glimmered with a shred of hope.

He shook his head. "She's not for you."

Bummed, I said, "Okay, sir. Whatever you say."

I watched Josh as he stared at Janie and DD walking off the dock. I wondered if she remembered the name her mother had given her. As she turned the corner, I caught another glimpse of her smile. It was beautiful.

Josh started talking, but I wasn't entirely sure if he was talking to me or just speaking out loud.

"Seeing her was almost too painful to tolerate. I need to find a way to manage my emotions. Lizzie would be disappointed in me if I didn't try to build a relationship with Janie. I've missed her every day since the day Gray took her away."

It was unusual for Josh to be broody, but this was worse than normal. Staring out toward Hope in the distance, Josh said, "Did you see that dark-haired man following her?"

Wow. He's taking the papa bear thing to a whole new level. "I didn't see anything, man. You're sure you saw someone following her?"

"I could have sworn he was following her, but who knows. I'm out of whack right now."

Josh and I continued cleaning Mrs. Donahue's yacht in silence. He preferred the silence, and I enjoyed being on the dock with him. The additional income I earned helping Josh on the side helped me pay my bills.

I was twenty-four and on my own. My parents were wealthy socialites who traveled around the world and currently lived in France. I still lived in my childhood home that my parents owned in Southport. I took care of the house, and they let me live there. Randy and Renee are the ones who raised me.

"Ahhh," Josh scoffed. "I'm a fool." He slapped his brush onto the dock. Frustration consumed him. "I need to figure out how I can see Janie."

I stopped what I was doing and opened my mouth to speak, but he cut me off again.

"I know. I know. Her name is Hope."

I raised my eyebrow and snapped my mouth shut. That wasn't what I was going to say, but now wasn't the time.

"How do I spend time with her without my throat feeling like I'm sucking on a fire stick?"

I didn't know what to say. Josh had never shared his personal life before. "She's your wife's daughter. Just talk to her."

Josh cackled. "Oh, like you talk to her, Mr. Casanova."

"Fair point."

"I have so many questions, so much I want to share with her. I want to get to know her, my little girl. My Lizzie's little girl. At the same time, the pain is immense. Thinking about seeing her again makes my lungs tighten like they might collapse. Every time I look at her, I see Lizzie, and the pain is more than I can bear." He smacked his brush against the dock again.

"Okay, man. It's gonna be all right."

"Let's call it a day. I need to clear my head," Josh said as he started to pack up our supplies.

"You promised Mrs. Donahue we'd finish her boat today."

"I'll finish later. I need to be alone."

"But she's paying us a lot of money. Her boat needs to be done today," I grumbled.

"Noah," Josh yelled. "I said I'd freaking finish it later. Shit, man."

My shoulders slumped, and I exhaled. "You're being sort of an ass. I'll just finish the boat." I put my fingers up into air quotes and said, "You go clear your head."

"Great," Josh grunted and briskly walked toward his boat. I could hear him mumbling. "Don't think about Janie. Don't think about Janie. Don't think about Janie." He climbed onboard, and I chased after him.

"Josh wait," I yelled. I climbed onto his boat and sat in the first available seat. "Sit. Talk to me. I know I'm a lot younger, but you clearly have some demons you need to let loose. So go ahead. Let them loose on me."

Josh balled his fists and spoke through gritted teeth. "I swore to myself that I would wrap my hands around Catalina's neck and choke the very life out of her lungs if it was the last thing I did. Vengeance has kept me breathing for twenty years. Vengeance has kept my heart pumping blood through my veins like a steam engine barreling down the tracks." Josh paced as he spoke. "Catalina took everything from me, but worse, I allowed her to continue taking everything from me even after she vanished from the face of the earth. Now Janie..." He smacked his forehead each time he said her name. "Hope. Hope. Hope. I know her damn name is Hope."

He exhaled a breath and slumped down into the seat across from me. "Now, Hope is back, but Catalina isn't here. She can't ruin my life again. The only person who could screw me now is me." He jabbed his thumb into his chest and exhaled. "Janie, sweet baby, Janie all grown up as Hope, was standing in front of me on the dock, and I could barely form words."

Before I could even think about my reaction, I huffed. "I know the feeling."

Josh glared at me, and I shrank an inch.

I jerked back when he shouted, "Josh Miller, get up and get your shit together." He slammed his hand on the edge of the boat and continued shouting at himself. "Life just slapped you in the face with a second chance." He slowly put one foot in front of the other. He flung his hand in the air and didn't look back as he mumbled, "I'm taking a shower."

FIFTEEN

Hope

The birds were chirping outside the window as I pried my eyes open. I had my first official job working at Bayview Books. Curled under the covers in my new bed, I yawned and snuggled with DD. She plopped her head on my chest, silently requesting a scratch behind her ears. I ran my fingers up and down along her curls, and she fell into a rhythm of heavy breathing.

My mother's red notebook lit up like a beacon on my dresser. "What do you think DD? Should we read another entry?" She slapped her tail on the bed over and over. I guessed that meant yes. I reached across the bed until I wrapped my fingertips along the silver coils. I pulled the book toward me and laid it on the bed.

Often, I wondered what it would be like to know my mother, hold her hand, or hear her voice. I often asked myself what she would do in a situation. Now, I had this book that was a window into her soul, and every time I thought about reading her words, I had to work up the courage to look at the pages.

"Maybe another time, DD. We don't want to be late. It's our first day." I covered my ears to dull the barking. DD was running in circles on the bed and barking so loud she may have woken up every person on Caswell Avenue. "Okay, girl. Settle down. We'll read another entry, but just one." DD nestled in beside me as I opened the journal and began to read aloud.

Dear Janie Bug,

Today is your 2nd birthday, and your father hosted a party. He went all out. It was a party fit for royalty. All the Disney princesses attended. There were even pumpkin carriage rides and horses. You enjoyed every second of it. Your cute dimples were on full display because the smile never left your face.

Your father worked hard his entire life and amassed wealth beyond anything you can imagine. I'm not sure I want him to be part of your life, but he's your father and wants to love you. I want to give him the chance, but he hasn't wholly earned it yet. I also don't want you to be raised with a silver spoon in your mouth. You need to learn to work hard and earn your way. Life will beat you down, and you must know that you can take the blows, get back up, and move forward.

Mom's WOW – Words Of Wisdom

Work hard to achieve your dreams, whatever they may be. But always remember that you rise by lifting others. Be humble and kind. As Cornelius Plantinga said, "A humble person is more likely to be self-confident. A person with real humility knows how much they are loved."

Know that you can do anything you truly put your mind to and that you are loved and supported. Achieving great success will take a lot of work and sacrifice, but it will be worth it if you're chasing your dreams. No matter what you do, remember to stay humble and believe in yourself. When you begin your first job in the workforce, until the last, give it your all. Don't hesitate to take chances and do more of what you enjoy.

Love, Mom

I had no idea what I wanted to do with my life. I barely understood who I was. I was born Janie Levine. Thanks to my dad's batshit crazy wife kidnapping me, I was Sophie Stone for a brief time. I've been Hope Miller, a ranch girl from Montana, for most of my life. My father is Grayson Stone, the intriguing, secretive billionaire who raised me.

Today, I'm Hope Miller, Ava Levine's long lost cousin and bookshop assistant. If I don't get moving, I'll be fired before I start.

I tied my hair into a messy bun and selected the best pair of tan cotton pants I owned. I topped them off with a green, V-neck T shirt and a black cardigan sweater. I glazed my lips with the gloss I had in my purse, grabbed my backpack, and headed to the bookstore. This was my first job working with someone other than my father's ranch hands, in-house cooks, or someone on his staff in general. Technically, I was still working for my family. I loved books, and I wanted to do a good job. Plus, I might get to see Noah. *Noah? Why am I thinking about Noah?*

DD wanted to come, but I was afraid to bring her on my first day. "I'm sorry, girl. You can't come yet." I patted her head. "I'll ask Ava today if she minds if you tag along while I'm working."

I couldn't help but wonder what life was like when my mom lived here. *Did she walk on this very street?* A gust of wind rustled up some leaves, chilling my spine. I shivered as I quickened my pace and hustled to the bookstore.

I rubbed my hands up and down my arms as I walked through the front door. "You're right on time," Ava said. "You can put your bag in the staff room or behind the front counter. We have a new pile of books to shelve."

I walked behind the counter and tucked my bag into an open cubby. "I'm ready to jump right in. Just point me in the proper direction."

Ava was a few inches taller than me and very slender. A pencil was tucked behind her ear, holding her wavy auburn hair which hung down the middle of her back, out of her face. I stood behind the counter for a moment and observed her. She seemed happy and content. At the very least, she seemed to own her position at the bookstore. I was barely comfortable acknowledging my real name.

I took a deep breath and exhaled my fears. Stepping out from behind the counter, I said, "I'm ready. Where do you want me?"

Ava pointed to a stack of boxes beside a bookcase marked historical fiction. "See those boxes? We need to unpack the books in them and put them alphabetically on the shelf right there." She pointed to an empty shelf near the stack of boxes.

I ripped open the top of the box, and the most glorious smell danced into my nostrils. I inhaled deeply, almost sucking the pages up my nose. "I just love the smell of fresh books," I said as I looked at Ava. I didn't want her to think I was some kind of weirdo.

"Me, too," Ava said as she danced around the aisle, pulling one book at a time from the box.

A book with flowers on the cover reminded me of something. "Ava, thank your parents for the flowers. I got a beautiful vase of flowers welcoming me to Southport. The card didn't say who they were from, but I assumed it was them."

Her eyes drifted upward as she searched her memory for the answer. "I don't think they're from my folks. They would have mentioned it. You'd have to ask them to be sure. I'm thinking maybe someone else was welcoming you to town." She giggled.

I shrugged. "I have no idea who else they'd be from."

"Ooohh," Ava said. "You have a secret admirer."

I rolled my eyes but was diverted to the song playing over the speakers. "What's this song?"

Ava gasped. "You don't know Taylor Swift? She was all the rage back in the day when our parents were young. Her fans were called Swifties." Ava fluffed her hair. "I would have been a total Swifty back then."

"Okay, yeah. I've heard of Taylor Swift. I just haven't listened to much of her music. My father played mostly classical music. You know, like Chopin and Beethoven. Occasionally, I'd get a little Scott Joplin ragtime." I pulled a few books from the box and placed them onto the shelf. "Are you familiar with ragtime?"

Ava looked dumbfounded. I wasn't sure if it was because I didn't know the Taylor Swift song, or she had never heard of ragtime. Either way, I wanted to get off the topic of music as quickly as possible. Hoping to change the subject, I said, "Tell me what it was like to grow up here?"

She beamed "Southport is the best. I couldn't imagine growing up anywhere else."

"Do you ever want to leave? Like, go find yourself." I held a book in my hand titled Hawaii 1948. "Hawaii?" I turned the cover toward Ava.

"I wouldn't mind visiting Hawaii." She lifted her arms into the air and did a little hula dance. "The owner asked me to grab some travel books. She wanted Hawaii, New York, and Montana." Ava took the book from my hands. "The cover's beautiful."

I opened my mouth to tell her about all the fantastic things about Montana, but I paused. "It sure is pretty." My natural instinct was to tell her how beautiful Kaffi ranch was, but I didn't. I wasn't ready to trust anyone yet. Also, my father would lecture me about giving away our home's location.

Ava was breaking down the boxes when a voice called from the front door. "Ava. I'm here." Recognizing the smooth tone, my stomach did a cartwheel.

"It's Noah. I think he has a major crush on you." Ava playfully poked my shoulder with her finger.

I drew my eyebrows in and wrinkled my forehead. "No, he doesn't. He doesn't even know me." I tried to sound uninterested, but I could feel the heat rising inside, turning my cheeks red.

Ava covered her mouth, her eyes going wide. "Oh my God. You have a crush on him, too!"

Just then, Noah turned the corner. "Um. Did I interrupt something?"

Ava burst out laughing, and I held the Hawaii travel book out like it could shield me from the moment.

"I'm sorry I'm a little late. You can go now if you need to. I'll close," he said, glancing at Ava, his tone casual but his eyes flickering with curiosity.

"It's okay, Noah. My plans got canceled, so I'll hang out here for the night." Ava smiled. She was clearly enjoying the moment.

SIXTEEN

Hope

A young woman entered the bookstore with her daughter.

"Hello, welcome to Bayview Books," I said. "How can I help you?"

The woman smiled. "We're here to check out some books upstairs and hang in the pirate ship." She and her little girl bee-bopped up the stairs.

Ava said, "Let us know if you need anything."

Noah and I went back to work cleaning the bookshelves. He animatedly launched into a discussion about the book he just finished. The main character, Levi, was a math professor who discovered time travel formulas. I zoned out somewhere around theoretical time dilation. An adorable glimmer in his eye warmed my heart as he continued about Einstein's theory of relativity and how mass and energy are interconnected.

"I love math," I said. "Abstract Algebra was my favorite."

Noah's smile widened. "Abstract Algebra is amazing! I mean, the algebraic structures and how the sets work with specific operations—it's just mind-blowing! It's so different from the number systems we're used to, you know."

I couldn't believe the words coming out of his mouth. My heart raced as he spoke, and my stomach fluttered. I was so excited I practically shouted, "Like groups, rings, fields, and modules." Unable to contain my energy, I jumped up. "And vector spaces, lattices, and algebras over a field!"

"You think you understand math, and then Abstract Algebra comes along and says, just kidding. You don't know shit." Noah flicked his hand dismissively as a playful grin spread across his face. His enthusiasm lit up his eyes and blended his smartness with a charmingly nerdy appeal.

"You two are insane." Shaking her head in disbelief, Ava chimed in, "I thought Noah was the only person in existence who got excited about math, but I guess there are two of you now."

"Math is beautiful. If you understand it, you can see it everywhere," I said with my hands clasped over my chest as I looked toward the ceiling. My eyes fluttered shut as I envisioned the elegant formulas swirling around me, like constellations in a night sky.

"Noah, wipe the drool off your face," Ava teased.

He chuckled and shook his head as she playfully jostled his shoulders. "Whatever, Ava. It's not every day you meet someone who appreciates math the way I do."

"You guys are silly," I said with a grin. "Math and books are my love language."

"Great," Ava said. "Let's put your skills to good use then. You can count the money drawer while Noah and I go through the closing procedures."

I stacked all the bills facing the same direction, counted the money, and followed the examples in the binder to document everything. The money count matched perfectly on my first try.

"Done," I shouted.

"Excellent. We are, too," Ava said.

I raised my hand to high-five Noah and said, "Goodbye. Have a great night."

Noah shook his head, a playful grin spreading across his face. "We're math buddies now." He reached his arm around my waist and pulled me into a side hug. I leaned in, only to awkwardly bump my head against his shoulder. *Great, Hope. Smooth move.*

Noah laughed. "Oh no, are you okay?" He pressed a gentle kiss to my forehead and rubbed the spot where I'd bumped him, his touch sending a flutter of warmth through me.

"Okay, love birds, it's time to go," Ava said.

"We aren't love birds," I insisted, my cheeks flushing from that forehead kiss. "We're math buddies."

Noah and I exchanged one last smile and a goodbye before I zipped up my coat and started walking down Moore Street. The warmth of our brief moment together took the chill of the evening air.

"I told Mom I'd grab some things from the general store on the way home," Ava said as she pointed across the street.

"I really should let DD out. You okay if I go ahead?"

"Of course. I'll see you later." She disappeared down the street.

I couldn't stop smiling as I walked. I successfully finished my first day at the bookstore. I genuinely liked working with Ava, and being at the store somehow helped me feel closer to my mother than ever. If I were being honest with myself, I also enjoyed getting to know Noah, and the fact that he likes books and math made him even hotter.

Suddenly, my euphoria shattered as I heard footsteps from behind. I darted through Hidden Treasure's front door and slipped out the side.

He followed me, a dead giveaway. *Amateur.*

When Ava, Noah, and I left the bookstore for the night, I had spotted a man in a black jacket leaning against the building across the street. It didn't hit me at first who he was, but now his face was clear as day in my mind. He was the same man I had seen standing outside my car the other day. He must be the one responsible for the footsteps I heard following me.

I ducked inside the Christmas House and weaved through the crowd. The store was crowded with people, and gigantic bows of different Christmas ribbons hung from the walls. I spotted an exit door and lunged toward it. I ran out of the back and around the street and then tucked behind a large bush. I slowed my breath and waited.

A few minutes later, I watched as the man in the black jacket stepped onto the road. He looked around, paused, and then looked around again before he walked toward me. I was confident he couldn't see me, but I crouched lower to be safe. Again, I waited.

He inched closer. I closed my eyes, inhaled a full breath, and remembered my training. Just as he approached, I spun low to the ground with my leg out and knocked him on his back. Before he even figured out what had happened, I flattened my hand and karate-chopped his throat, and then I drove the heel of my palm upward into his nose. Blood dripped down his lips.

I pressed my foot against his neck and demanded, "Who are you? Why are you following me?"

He didn't respond.

I pressed my foot harder into his throat, but he remained silent, his eyes closed.

Shit! Did I kill him?

Holding my breath, I tried not to panic. Leaning over the man, I pressed two fingers into his neck. He had a pulse. *Thank God. He's unconscious, not dead.* I did my best to drag him into the bushes. I certainly didn't want to stick around to find out if he had any friends. Hopefully, people walking past would assume he had passed out from too many drinks and was sleeping it off in the bush.

SEVENTEEN

Montana - Past

Hope

Bang.

The sound rang out across the open range and echoed through the hills. My earphones muffled the thunderous bang, but the sound was still deafening and sent vibrations pulsating through my body. The pumpkin splattered into a million pieces, and seeds, covered in slime, flew through the air.

"Good work, Hope," Bryce said as he patted my shoulder. I lay flat on the earth with the rifle flush against my right eye. The metal scope was cold as it touched my skin. Today's "life lesson" was sharpshooting.

I was officially sixteen now, and the time had come to put my training to the test. I overheard my father tell Bryce earlier today, "She needs to be able to protect herself in every way."

I had been shooting guns at a stationary target since I was six years old. When I was ten, Bryce started to take me hunting, where I learned to shoot at moving targets and bring dinner home.

Today, I learned to shoot a rifle and hit a target a thousand yards away. The furthest I'd ever tried. Bryce had been teaching me the art of the shot.

"There are several factors to consider, Hope. You need to give ample thought and consideration to all of them. Do you understand what I'm saying?" Bryce asked, his hulking frame towering above me. "If you're shooting at a person, you can aim for the head, but you typically only get one shot. If you miss, you must pack up and get the hell out of dodge. I recommend you aim for something larger to guarantee you make contact. I suggest you aim for one of the two triangles." He traced large triangles from his chest to his neck and then from his hip bones to his pelvis.

Brushing a strand of blonde air out of his eye, he said, "Being a sniper is about patience and steadiness."

Somehow, my gut alerted me that shooting a 338 Sniper Rifle wasn't normal; it was my life. I had spent the last fifteen years on a ranch in the middle of nowhere, being raised by my father, his ranch hands, a teacher, and my father's henchmen. Nothing about my world was normal. I wasn't sure I had enough life experience to know what normal was, but I had enough experience to know how I was living wasn't it.

Bang.

I fired another shot, and the sound bellowed across the field. Once again, the pumpkin exploded, and pumpkin guts splattered everywhere. I chuckled. "Louisa would be so pissed if she knew we were using her prize pumpkins for target practice." According to Bryce, they were the perfect size.

"Louisa will understand." He packed his gun. "You're a natural. Tomorrow, we'll do target practice with handguns." He grabbed my hand and helped me off the ground. "Go clean the gun and lock it back in the case," he said as I brushed the grass off my stomach.

I charged through the front door. "Gray! I'm back," I shouted as I ran up the stairs to my room. I was meeting Gabe at the barn to finish Moby Dick. We only had a few chapters left.

"Don't call me Gray. I'm your father," I heard him yell from his office.

"Yes, Father," I replied with a bit of extra snark.

I changed into a purple sports bra and black running shorts. "I'm going for a run," I said, standing in the doorway of my father's office.

"Okay, don't be too long. Geoffrey will have dinner ready in about an hour." He looked up at me. "Aren't you forgetting something?"

Confused, I furrowed my brow. "Not sure what you mean."

"Your clothes. How about a shirt or something?"

"Seriously, Gray." I rolled my eyes. "Who's going to see me or even care what I'm wearing?"

"Damn it, Hope. I'm your father." He ran his fingers through his hair and then slammed them onto his desk. "Stop calling me Gray."

I stomped out. I didn't care. What was he going to do? Send me away? Where would he send me? He was afraid to let me out into the big evil world. I rolled my eyes at the thought.

I ran the entire mile from the house to the barn. This way, I wasn't lying; technically, I did go for a run. When I arrived, my skin glistened with sweat. Gabe was pacing the barn, kicking the hay with his steps. His skin looked perfect in the sunlight that poured through the slits on the roof. His muscles sculpted his frame so perfectly. I ran into his arms. He held my face in his hands and kissed the top of my head.

"I thought you weren't going to come," he whispered. His breath tickled my ear as he spoke.

"I'm sorry. Bryce took me sharpshooting, and it took forever to get back. Then I had a little spat with my father."

He wove his fingers between mine and led me up the stairs to the barn loft. A few years ago, we made a reading spot up there.

Gabe stashed a lantern, blankets, and pillows, and I brought several books. Over the years, I taught Gabe how to read, but he still liked it when I read aloud to him.

"You look beautiful, Hope," he said as he lay on the blanket.

My skin got hot, and my stomach fluttered. I was uncomfortable with this feeling. "Gabe, you're my best friend. I don't know what I'd do without you." I lay beside him and rested my head on his chest.

"Hope." I loved the way he said my name. "You're my best friend, too. I want to kiss you now. Is that okay with you?"

I looked into his eyes and smiled. His lips gently graced mine, and his hand cupped my breast. I leaned into his kiss and pulled him closer to me. I quickly pulled my mouth from his and bit my bottom lip.

"Is everything okay?" He rolled on his side to face me and ran his fingertip along my abdomen.

"Everything is perfect. That was perfect." I put my hand in his.

Gabe smiled. "Can we do that again sometime?"

"Yes, but I don't trust myself to stay in control." I kissed his lips. "When I'm ready, I'll let you know. Until then, I think we should stick to books."

He looked disappointed, but kissed my forehead and said, "Okay, Hope. I'll wait."

EIGHTEEN

Montana - Past

Hope

The sound of my breath filled the space around me. The silence was so deafening that I swore the rise and fall of my chest made a sound. I stood poised behind a large oak tree. A bead of sweat slid from my brow down my cheek in the darkness.

Hinata was on the hunt, and I needed to escape. I closed my eyes like I had been taught. I steadied my breath and listened. A bird called out in the distance. The leaves rustled.

I waited. Calm and cool, I stood at the ready, listening for any sign of Hinata.

Then, I heard it.

A faint crackling sound, possibly fifty yards to my right. I opened my arms and sprang into action. Rolling to the ground, I crawled along the earth on my belly toward my prey. A twinge of excitement mixed with fear came over me as I spotted the tip of Hinata's boots about a dozen yards away. I rolled behind another oak tree, clambered to my feet, and climbed. "Height is your advantage, Hope. Whenever you can have the high ground, take it," Hinata's voice echoed in my head.

I climbed slowly and purposefully until I could steady myself on a thick branch. Clinging to the tree with my right arm, I drew my gun with my left hand. I leaned my body against the massive oak tree and aimed. Adjusting the scope, I let out a calming breath while I gathered my prey in my sight.

Hinata stood oblivious, camouflaged in the wilderness, but I saw his boot and was certain it was him. I closed my eyes once again and inhaled a large gulp of oxygen. I opened my eyes and slowly exhaled, squeezing the trigger. Birds scattered from the trees, and animals ran frantically through the woods as the shot rang out and connected with my target. I finally beat my master. The student had out maneuvered the teacher.

I scurried down the tree and ran toward him. "Hin. Hin." I laughed. "I got you. I got you this time."

Silence.

"Hin," I shouted.

Silence.

It was a paint bullet. Surely, he's fine. Right? My heart skipped a beat.

"Hin?"

When I approached, Hin was lying on his back, unconscious. Blue paint was splattered across his shiny black hair and dripped down his face, making his skin look more yellow than normal.

My father had security at the ready all over the country, but four guards lived here year-round. Hinata was my favorite. He was a master in several martial arts. He could kill someone with his bare hands, although he was incredibly gentle and kind.

Four days a week for as far back as I could remember, he took me out to the pasture and trained me in Karate and Tai Chi. Every lesson, he'd instruct me to take my shoes off. "You must be grounded in the earth, Hope," he'd say. "Become one with the Creator. Feel the connection through your feet." As I got older, I understood and came to appreciate that connection. Hinata was so wise. Steady and safe, he didn't rattle easily.

Shaking him, I said, "Hin. Hin. Wake up." Firmly, I pressed my hands into his shoulder and shook him again. "Come on, Hin. This isn't funny anymore. Wake up." I was now screaming at the top of my lungs.

I pressed two fingers against his neck to search for a pulse. I exhaled a sigh of relief when I felt his heartbeat coursing through his veins.

"Hin!" I shouted again.

"Damn, Hope. You don't have to yell." His eyes slowly blinked open. He leaned on one elbow and put his other hand on his head. "You hit me square in the head. Knocked me out."

I stared wide-eyed. I wasn't aiming for his head. "I'm sorry. Are you okay?"

"You could have killed me."

"I know. I'm sorry." Suddenly exhausted, I slumped over.

He took his hand from his head and held it up. "Give me five."

I drew my eyebrows down in confusion. "Huh?"

"You tracked for me ten miles, found the high ground, and hit your target. I'm so freaking proud of you. You've officially earned the title of professional tracker." I slapped his hand with mine and smiled. "The youngest professional tracker I know."

At the ripe old age of seventeen, I was a professional tracker. A grin stretched across my face. I had trained with Hinata my entire life. My father wanted to ensure I could read a room, spot an attacker, and defend myself. After all these years, my teacher thought I was ready.

"Tomorrow's your final test," Hin said as I helped him to his feet. "I'm taking you into town for a real-life scenario." He took a rag from his pocket and began wiping the paint from his head and face. "You'll need to manage to get into a disguise, steal a car, and escape from an attacker or possibly attackers. And you'll need to do all of this without drawing any attention."

"I'm ready. I was trained by the best." I lifted my chin in the air with my hands on my hips.

Hinata chuckled. "Okay. We'll see. Let's not get too cocky."

NINETEEN

Montana - Past

Hope

Girty was a little extra fickle today. She didn't want to give up her egg. Flapping her brown and red wings, she squawked as I approached. "It's okay Girty girl. You know me," I reassured her as I attempted to collect her egg. Every morning after I mucked the stalls, I trotted down to the hen house and collected the eggs for Geoffrey.

Walking back from the chicken coop, I was listening to classical music on my iPod when I heard Betty the cow let out a scream so horrific it made my blood curdle. Jo, our veterinarian, was leaning over her. I set the eggs down and ran toward them. Jo was built like a brick shit house, and she was all business most of the time.

She was the veterinarian, but she was also part of the security team. I spent a few days a week with her learning how to care for the animals. My father hoped I could manage the ranch someday, but I had different plans.

Jo's long, curly brown hair was tied up in a messy bun that looked like a bird's nest sitting on her head. "What's happening, Jo? Is everything ok?"

"Come, Hope. Help," she shouted. Never taking her eyes off Betty, she said. "Betty's gone into labor."

"How? It's not time." I hurried to Jo's side.

"She collapsed, and I think the calf is coming." Jo's hands were covered in bloody goop.

I knelt beside her. "What can I do?"

"Put your hands here and press down," she said as she placed my hands on Betty. I pressed down with all my might to create a small opening.

"Good. Keep pressing," Jo urged, her hands working inside Betty. I turned my gaze away, discomfort pooling in my stomach. "I can feel it. I'm right there," she said through gritted teeth.

Jo tugged with all her might and fell onto her back. The baby calf practically flopped on top of her. She was covered in gunk and goop. I squeezed my eyes shut. I didn't want to take in the scene.

"Gross," I said as I tried to flick fetal matter off my hands. My nose wrinkled, and my lips twisted in disgust.

"Oh, you'll survive," Jo said, rolling her eyes. "You just helped bring a new life into this world."

I hadn't thought about that, but I guess I did. Betty let out a painful mooing sound. She was losing a significant amount of blood. At least, it seemed that way, but maybe it was normal.

"Shit," Jo shouted. "Shit, shit, shit." She was frantically running around Betty doing doctorly things as I stood there like a deer in headlights. Betty's calf was finding her feet and working hard to stand up, oblivious to what was happening with her mother. "Hand me those clamps." Jo pointed to a bag full of tools and supplies.

I dug through the bag until I found what looked to be a clamp and handed it to Jo. She gripped it tightly and plunged her hands back inside Betty. The moment she did, Betty moaned and reared her head up off the ground. "Got it," Jo said. "Whew."

She pulled her hands out of Betty and wiped them on her shirt. "It's going to be okay girl. You're going to be okay." Jo knelt down by the cow and gently caressed her head. "Everything's going to be okay."

I stood without words, motionless.

"What shall we name her?" Jo said.

"How about Boop." I laughed.

"Boop, it is."

"I'm sorry I'm late. I was helping Jo. Betty had her calf today," I said as I took my shoes off.

"Let's get right to it. You've already wasted twenty minutes of my time," Hinata said.

"Damn. Slow your roll. I was helping Jo. It's not like I was goofing off." I stood in the ready position.

"Enough chatter. Let's begin."

The blades of grass were pleasant on the bottoms of my feet. As I grounded into the earth, I was instantly at peace. I closed my eyes and inhaled slowly and then exhaled. With each movement, my body and breath became one. Strong, slow movements in repetition.

Hin and I practiced for years to master the movements. I was grateful for Hinata and his teaching. On the one hand, he trained my body to be a weapon, but on the other hand, he trained me to tap into my inner peace and strength. Sidestep, swipe. Breathe in and out. Step back, kick, and hold. Find the earth and breathe.

I can't imagine life without learning his teachings. I cherished Hinata's lessons. Now twenty-two years old with a master's degree in advanced mathematics and an additional degree in psychology, my father finally allowed me to choose how to spend my time.

He said, "You've learned all the lessons, you have two degrees, and I believe you can finally protect yourself. Leaving the ranch is unsafe, but I permit you to choose how you spend your time."

Yippee. I could choose how to spend my time. Sarcastic thoughts oozed from my pores. I was suffocating in this place. My entire life had been on this farm. I wanted to explore the world. I wanted to meet my family. Why did my father share so many stories about my mother and her family if he never planned to let me meet them? He thought he was being so kind. *"Hope, aren't I wonderful? After twenty-two years, I'm letting you decide how to spend your time."*

I understood that some lunatic killed my mother. According to his stories, she kidnapped me twice and would stop at nothing to ruin our lives and find me. I believed him, but I was tired of feeling trapped. Montana was my home, and our ranch was beautiful. Most kids would be ecstatic to grow up in such a place.

But I was ready for more. I longed to meet my family and experience the world beyond these wide-open spaces. As I gazed out at the horizon, I realized it was time to take control of my own story.

TWENTY

Hope

The past few days working with Ava and Noah at the bookstore have been great, but I was glad to have a day off. The man with the black jacket hadn't reappeared, or he had become better at staying invisible. I didn't tell anyone about my encounter with him that night. Considering a girl beat him up, I assumed he wouldn't tell anyone, either.

I stepped out of my apartment and tapped Uncle Randy's back door. The delicious smell of freshly cooked bacon smacked me in the face as I entered. My mouth salivated instantly. Renee was frolicking around the kitchen, placing various serving dishes on the island. Every dish has a Christmas theme, pattern, or color.

Randy and Ava said, "Hello" in unison.

"Hi. Smells amazing," I said.

DD trotted in behind me. Renee stopped cutting the cantaloupe, bent over, and patted her on the head. "Hello, DD. Here's a special treat I saved just for you," she said in a sweet, childish tone.

Renee handed me a basket of strawberries. "Can you cut this, please?"

"Sure."

I snagged the cutting board from under the counter and started cutting the strawberries, placing them in a white bowl with a Christmas tree in the center.

"How are things going at the bookstore?" Randy said.

I opened my mouth to reply but hesitated. Once again, I was caught off guard when I saw Randy in all his Christmas glory. He rocked a green pair of sweatpants, a candy cane covered short sleeve T-shirt, an apron that looked like Santa Claus in a speedo, and brown Crocs.

"The bookstore's pretty awesome." I raised my eyebrows. "But not as awesome as your outfit."

Renee snorted and laughed so hard that tears welled up in her eyes.

Pointing to Ava, I said, "My boss is fantastic."

Everyone laughed as Ava said, "It's been great to have the extra help."

Randy cracked the eggs into a red bowl with holly leaves around the edges and began mixing in the milk and cheese. *Geez, even the mixing bowl is Christmas.*

DD barked just before we heard a knock at the door. An older man and a woman strolled in.

Renee ran to the door, took both of their coats, and gave them each a hug. *So much hugging, I'm not used to all the hugging.* My stomach tightened, and my skin started to tingle. I suddenly felt out of place.

The woman gasped when she saw me. Clasping her hands together, she said, "Hope! You look just like your mother. I loved your mom. She was an incredible lady. She loved my bookstore."

"Thank you. You must be Helen," I said.

She charged toward me, wrapped her arms around me, and squeezed so tight I thought I might never draw another breath. "Oh, Janie. Janie, my girl. I'd given up hope. I thought we'd never see you again." A tear trickled down her cheek.

She released me, put her hands on my shoulders, and looked me up and down to assess every inch of me.

"I prefer Hope." I didn't know what to say. I didn't share their feelings. I wanted to get to know this side of my family, but I couldn't make myself feel how they did. "I'm happy to be here, but the reunion is a bit overwhelming."

Randy said, "It's okay, kiddo. Just take it one day at a time."

DD jumped off the couch and stood by Helen's side. She rubbed her leg with her head and then used her nose to flip her hand on top of her head. I appreciated the distraction because it pulled the attention away from me. *DD to the rescue.*

Helen sat on the couch and called DD to follow her. She began rubbing DD behind the ears. "No pressure, Hope. We're all just glad you're here."

After introducing himself, Drew sat on the couch next to Helen and began to pet DD on the back. She was getting spoiled with all this attention.

Helen was beaming when she said, "I have so many questions."

"We all do," Randy said. "But Hope will tell us when she's ready."

"How's your dad?" Helen asked. Renee shot her a fierce look. "What? I can't ask how Gray is?"

"My father's fine. He made sure I was safe, well-educated, and prepared to protect myself."

"What does that mean?" Helen said.

Randy raised his spatula and shouted from the kitchen, "All right. All right. Enough questions. Give us an update on the historical society."

Renee was putting food on the table and said, "Yes. Please update us, but let's do it at the table while we eat."

Everyone took a seat in the kitchen. Drew whispered to me as he walked by. "We're so glad you're here." He smiled and continued to his chair.

"There isn't much to tell. Drew and I are determined to keep Southport as the Southport it is. The big builders keep trying to push their way in, and we won't allow it." Helen scooped a pile of scrambled eggs onto her plate and covered them in ketchup. "We're working to get back some of the fun town events we used to hold. We're making some good progress there, which is nice."

"That's great," Renee said. "I miss the parades, especially the golf cart Christmas parade."

Ava turned to me and said, "The parades in Southport used to be epic. The whole town would either participate or watch from the curb, but everyone was there one way or another."

Renee laughed. "Your mom actually danced in the Christmas parade. She was dressed up like a snowman, face paint and all."

I chewed my food and imagined my mom dancing in the street during the Christmas parade. I wish I had those memories of her, that I could have shared those moments of going to a Southport parade with Her.

Randy said, "What are you girls doing today?"

Ava took a bite of her Burney's croissant and said, "I have to work today."

Helen smiled. "You're doing such a great job with the bookstore."

I could see how much her words meant to Ava. She beamed with pride.

Suddenly, a thought popped into my head. "I think I'm going to go fishing. I want to be alone on the water, just catching fish. Maybe we can eat them for dinner?"

Randy tapped his hand on the table. "A girl after my own heart. If you catch some fish, we'll definitely eat them. I'll filet them for you."

"Oh, I'll catch fish. I'll filet them, too. We can prep them together for dinner," I said.

"Fish for dinner it is."

DD and I strolled along Caswell Avenue to the water and headed toward the yacht basin. The day was beautiful. Full of clear blue skies as far as the eye could see. The sun beamed down onto the water, making it difficult to see. I had to squint if I didn't shield my eyes with my hand. I headed toward the boat rental stand, and DD followed behind. I tapped the bell on the counter with my fingertips a few times. An older gentleman wearing a fishing hat that flopped over his eyes appeared.

"How may I help you?" the man said.

"I'd like to rent a boat."

"I'm sorry, sweetie, we don't have any available today. We can rent you one tomorrow."

Disappointed, I said, "Thank you. I can't tomorrow. I'll try again another time."

As I turned to leave, I spotted a small tiller-steered boat anchored at the end of the dock. Silver letters painted along the army green hull read, "Maintenance Boat."

I hesitated and then strolled along the dock to get a closer look. With my fist clenched, I pumped my arm. "Yes!" The boat was identical to the one my father had on the ranch, and to my surprise, the keys were still in the ignition.

A rustling billowed from the bathroom, but when I looked around, the dock was empty.

I motioned for DD to jump in as I set my fishing pole inside the boat. I cranked the engine and took off like a shot. The clerk from behind the counter was jogging down the dock, waving his hands and yelling something I couldn't understand. A younger boy jumped onto a jet ski, but he couldn't get it started.

I laughed. "DD, we're criminals." She gave me a stank eye. "I'll take the boat back after catching a few fish."

Motoring as fast as the little tiller-steered motor would go, I barreled down the Intercoastal Waterway toward the bay. About five miles into the trip, I found a little cove and anchored the "borrowed" boat. DD was curled in a ball on the floor, sound asleep. It seems her conscience was unaffected by our crime.

Searching the boat, I found the anchor tucked beneath a seat and dropped it into the water. I cast my fishing rod into the water and waited while the sun beat down on my face.

Alone.

Regret bubbled up in my esophagus. "I should have told my father where I was going."

DD looked at me as though to say, "Yes. You should have."

I sighed. "He wouldn't understand." I reeled in my line and cast again. "I needed to find myself and my family. Southport was the best place to do that. Plus, I wouldn't have met you."

DD lifted her head and yawned.

In the distance, the soft, gentle hum of a motor approached. A sparkling white Sea Doo Wave Runner with a teal and black seat turned the corner into the cove and beelined directly toward us.

Through a bullhorn, the driver said, "I don't want any trouble. I'm just here to bring the boat back."

"Noah?"

"Hope. Is that you?"

He pulled the Sea Doo alongside the boat and threw me a rope. I tied it to the boat to secure his wave runner. "Hope. What on earth? You stole the boat?" He was even cuter when he was confused.

"I wanted to go fishing, but all the boats were rented. I saw the mechanic boat with the keys inside." I shrugged. "I didn't think anyone would mind if I borrowed it for a few hours."

Noah shook his head. He rose and swung a leg over the side of the boat. As he climbed aboard, he lost his balance, bumping into me and sent us both tumbling to the deck.

"Ugg," I said. Chest to chest, he was sprawled on top of me.

"I'm sorry. I'm so sorry," Noah said as he clambered to his feet. He reached out a hand to help me up. My foot was caught on something hooked under the seat, and I pulled him back onto me. We burst out laughing. Noah rolled over, and we both lay on our backs.

"Did you know it was me that took the boat?"

"I saw DD. Well, at least I thought it was DD."

"Am I in trouble?"

Noah rolled onto his side and propped his head with his arm. "I told Mr. Tucker at the dock I knew you, and I'd get you to bring the boat back. As long as you return the boat, everything will be fine." He poked his finger into my arm. "If you don't return the boat, I'll be responsible for replacing it."

I rolled toward him and smiled. "You vouched for me?"

His eyes connected with mine and I melted into a puddle of goo. "Of course, I did. You're my math buddy."

How could I forget? I'm the math buddy.

TWENTY ONE

Hope

Standing on the staircase, I stretched as far as I could to hang the white twinkling lights on the garland Ava had strung up. She said she was behind on decorating the store for Christmas. While Ava and I worked together on garland and lights on the staircase, Noah hung the holly and ribbon from the chandeliers. We had only an hour until the store opened. Ava expected a good crowd today because of the chess and checkers tournaments we were hosting. We needed to complete the decorations and clean up the store before opening at eleven.

"Did you hear I'm Southport's newest delinquent," I said, a teasing grin spreading across my face.

Crash!

A loud thud came from the center of the room, followed by a grunting sound. My heart dropped as Noah tumbled off the ladder.

"Oh my God, Noah. Are you okay?" Ava cried out. We both ran to his side.

Wearily, he muttered, "I'm okay. I reached a little too far and lost my balance." He stood slowly and twisted his torso from side to side. "I'm good. I promise. But maybe I'll call it a day on the chandeliers."

Ava laughed. "Delinquent, huh?" She arched an eyebrow, her expression turning mischievous. Noah's eyes darted between us, uncertainty flickering across his face.

Ava narrowed her eyes, jabbing her finger at Noah before switching her attention to me and back to him. "Wait a minute." Her frown deepened. "Do you know about this?"

Hooking the last strand of lights on the railing, I said, "I may have borrowed the maintenance boat at the dock."

Ava shot me a disappointed look.

"What?" I shrugged. "I wanted to go fishing, and it was the only boat available."

After I finished with the lights, I picked up the box of large red and green bows and began hanging them along the railing. "In my defense, the keys were in the ignition."

Noah jumped to my defense. "She didn't hurt anyone, and Mr. Tucker didn't mind. I talked to him. She brought the boat back in one piece. No harm, no foul." He looked at me and smiled.

"All right. I guess it's okay." Ava laughed. "I'm kidding. Of course, it's okay. I just wish I could've been there to see old Mr. Tucker's face when you drove off."

I finished putting the bows on the staircase, and Noah helped me clean up the decoration boxes. Ava was right. When the store opened, we had a flood of people. I manned the register and sold books, coffee, and pastries while Ava and Noah monitored the games.

I learned that Mr. Paul was the reigning chess champion, and Miss Tilly was the reigning checkers champion. Another elderly man was determined to dethrone Mr. Paul. He was not shy about saying so, and their emotions got heated. The intensity in the room could float a hot air balloon. I had never experienced anything like it.

Today was by far my busiest day at Bayview Books. I had my fill of people, and we still had a few hours left before the chaos died down. There was barely any time to keep up with the games because the register was hopping. I'd occasionally hear, "Take that or checkmate." Cheering and hollering increased in volume as the games continued. As each player was eliminated, they stayed to cheer on their favorite. I had no idea Bayview Books' Chess and Checkers Tournaments claimed such fervor.

Eddie, Mr. Paul's opponent today, gave him a run for his money, but Mr. Paul pulled through in the end. The champion lived on another day.

"What a mess," I said as I picked up the tenth half-full cup of hot chocolate. Napkins, plates, and crumbs were everywhere. I walked to the staff room to get the broom as Ava closed and locked the front door.

As I began sweeping, I said, "What do you think of me and Noah?"

Ava tied up her wavy red locks and walked behind the counter. "What do you mean?"

I sighed, frustration creeping into my voice. "What do you mean, *what do I mean*?" I stopped sweeping to give her my full attention.. "I mean Noah and me." I emphasized the words, hoping the added weight would help her understand my question better.

Noah walked over with a dustpan and placed it in front of the pile I created on the floor. "Let me help you," he said, his tone casual yet warm, a flicker of something more in his gaze.

I glanced at Ava. Heat crept into my cheeks as I felt my face flush.

She caught my eye and mouthed, "Oooohhhh," a teasing smile spreading across her lips.

Caught off guard, I blurted out, "I don't need your help." I immediately regretted my reaction when I saw Noah's expression falter. *Why did I say that?*

Sensing the tension, Ava chimed in, "Noah, I got some news on the Christmas Parade."

Ignoring my weird outburst, Noah emptied the dustpan into the trashcan. "Have they agreed to have the parade this year?"

"Not yet, but I'm hopeful. I think we're getting close," Ava said as she counted the money in the register.

I wanted to shout numbers to see if I could distract her. *What's wrong with me?* I let out a small chuckle. I couldn't help myself.

"What's funny?" Noah said.

"Nothing." I walked around the store, fluffed, and reorganized the couch pillows. I was surprised, but Noah left me alone. He didn't push for an answer to my laugh.

Ava put all the money into a bank bag and stuffed it into her backpack. "You heard about the Christmas Parade the other day at breakfast. The golf cart parade was such a fun time."

I had moved on to wiping down the tables and cleaning the chess pieces. "Sounds like a great time. Why did they stop having the parades?"

Ava and Noah glanced at each other. "About five years ago, two of the golf cart drivers had a little too much to drink, and they crashed into each other. One of the passengers fell out of the cart, was run over, and died. It was awful, so the mayor canceled all future parades, and they haven't been allowed since."

"That's terrible," I said. "How sad."

"It was awful, but the town loves the parades and wants to bring them back."

TWENTY TWO

Hope

After leaving the bookstore, I took the long way home. When I had the time, I preferred the long way because I never tired of the massive oak trees. Royal James, the local bar, was packed to the gills, with standing room only when I passed. I wandered aimlessly and eventually found myself at a picnic table on the water. Waves softly slapped against the rocks, creating a soothing symphony that was perfect for my soul.

I weaved my fingers together, placed them on the table, and rested my head in my hands. Facing the sun, I watched as the boats slowly moved by. Seagulls dove into the water, trying to snatch up their dinner. I took several diaphragmatic breaths to center myself. *What was I doing here? What did I expect to get out of my runaway trip to Southport?* I can't believe I'm admitting how I feel to myself, but I missed Montana. I missed my horses and the chickens. I missed my father. I even missed my teachers, all of them.

Suddenly, a voice said, "Janie?"

I stiffened.

"I'm sorry. I mean Hope."

I sat up and glanced over at the man. "Do I know you?"

The man appeared to be in his mid-fifties and very attractive. I'd remember if I'd seen him before. He pointed at the bench on the other side of the table. "May I?"

"It's a free country." My tone made it clear I didn't want to be bothered. I swiped a strand of hair out of my face and began to put my head back down on the table.

"Maybe you don't recognize me. It's Josh. Josh Miller."

I instantly felt like someone had punched me in the stomach. He looked like a completely different person. As I looked at him, a repulsive feeling swept through my body. I literally just had a moment of attraction for my mother's husband, my stepfather. I wanted to rinse my eyes out with paint thinner. Although the attraction was fleeting, it was nonetheless a moment. *Gag!*

"Have you read any of your mother's journal?"

"I have." I didn't know what to say or how to react. I was not equipped for the many feelings flowing through my body and putting my emotions on overdrive.

"She loved you, Janie. She loved you so much." His voice cracked.

My emotions exploded out of my mouth like projectile vomit. "My fucking name is Hope."

I stood up from the table and turned to walk away.

"Hope. Wait," he called. "I'm sorry. This is hard for me, too." He hurried to catch up.

"Leave me alone. I don't know you. You took a shower, cut your hair, and shaved your beard. Good for you, man. I don't want anything to do with you. You're the reason my mother died. It's your fault."

I could see the devastation in his eyes. My words cut deep into his soul. I wished I could take them back, but it was too late. He grabbed my wrist and stuffed a small piece of paper into my hand. "Here's my cell phone number. I'd love to talk and get to know you some time. When you're ready."

I turned in silence and walked home.

DD was standing at the front door when I arrived. Her tail wagged furiously. "Hello, DD," I said as I rubbed her face. She followed me to the kitchen, where she waited to receive her treat. "Were you a good girl today?" She sat on her hind legs, still and patient and stared at her reward. "I bumped into Josh today." She took off like a shot and zoomed around the house. "I'm glad you're excited. I didn't have the same reaction."

DD finally settled onto the couch and curled herself into a little ball. I picked up the red notebook from my coffee table and turned to the next entry.

Dear Janie Bug,

The past two days were the worst of my entire life. You were taken from us again, and I didn't think my heart could take it. I already lost you once. I couldn't lose you again. The town of Southport is a magical place with the most incredible people. Everyone came together to find you, and it was unbelievable. I was so grateful. I don't think I can let you out of my sight ever again, so when you get older, if you feel like I was a helicopter mom, now you'll know why. I love you so much, Janie Bug; my heart is so full with you in my life. Every day, I feel blessed to be your mother.

Mom's WOW – Words Of Wisdom

Life will be painful. I wish I could tell you otherwise. As parents, we do our best to shield and protect our children from this harsh reality, but life *will be* painful. However, when you accept that painful things are part of life, you understand that you can get through them and appreciate the immense good and joy surrounding you.

Let go of the pain and learn to forgive. Forgiveness is essential for your heart and living your best life. Holding on to anger or hatred only makes your life more painful. Mahatma Gandhi said, "The weak can never forgive. Forgiveness is the attribute of the strong." You are strong, Janie Bug. You are already so strong. No matter what you do, promise your mama you'll learn to forgive.

Love, Mom

I leaned back onto the couch, my mother's journal open across my chest. I held it like it was alive. I closed my eyes and imagined what it would be like to sit and talk with my mother, how I would tell her about my day and work through my problems with her.

I pulled the crinkled piece of paper out of my pocket and unfolded it. Then, I punched the number into my phone and began texting Josh.

Me: I'm sorry I was rude

My breath caught in my throat as I saw three dots appear

Josh: I understand. It's okay

Me: Do you still want to get together and talk?

Josh: I'd love that

Me: How about lunch tomorrow?

Josh: Perfect. Let's meet at the Pizza Café around noon

Me: See ya there

DD looked at me, and I swear she smiled.

TWENTY THREE

Hope

Two, three, five, seven. My hands were clammy, and my throat was dry. *Eleven, thirteen, Seventeen, nineteen.* I'd already tried on five different outfits. I don't know why I even cared. It was lunch with Josh Miller. *Big deal.* T*wenty-three, twenty-nine, thirty-one.* A dress seemed a little too formal, jeans were too casual, and sweatpants would be sloppy. I sighed and continued counting prime numbers in my head. Finally, I settled on a short, ruffly jean skirt, a crème sweater, and cowgirl boots. I checked myself over in the mirror. I was ready to have lunch with the guy who was almost your father. Patting DD on the head, I handed her a treat and grabbed my purse.

"Who am I kidding, DD? I'm not ready. I'm a nervous wreck." My palms were sweaty, and a giant lump took up residence in my throat. *Maybe I should cancel. What if he doesn't like me? What if he does?* I flopped down onto the couch and put my head in my hands. "What if we never get along?" I expelled a puff of air, and my bottom lip curled out. DD scratched at the door.

"Do you need to go outside, girl?" She tapped the door with her paw again. "Okay, DD. Just a sec." I opened the door, and she darted across the lawn and into the road. "DD! No! Stop!"

She paused, looked back at me, and then began to saunter down the road. "DD. Get back here." She acted like she didn't hear me and continued walking. "Okay. Okay. We'll go meet Josh." DD started a series of jump circles and tail wagging.

We approached the Pizza Café on Howe Street, and every fiber of my being was screaming to run away. I ignored my inner monologue and put my hand to the door handle. Josh was sitting by himself at the table in the corner. His hands were folded on top of the red and white checkered tablecloth. I walked through the door, and DD followed. Every place in Southport was pretty cool about having your pet in tow. Josh saw us and immediately stood and waved. He pulled out a chair for me to sit. I nodded. "Thank you."

"I'm glad you came. I wasn't sure you would," he said.

I pressed my lips together and looked down toward the table, the wood grain blurring as I fought against the rush of emotions swirling inside me. "I wasn't sure I'd come either."

Devon, at least that's what her nametag said, brought us water and menus. I wanted to climb under the table where I could hide from the flood of feelings that were threatening to overwhelm me.

Every day, some new emotion attacked my nervous system, and it was becoming too much to bear.

Josh laid down his menu and took a sip of water as if it could steady him. "Hope, I'm unsure what to say or where to start. But I'd like us to get to know each other."

I leaned over to peek under the table to check on DD, and she was resting her head on Josh's thigh as he petted her. "Looks like you made a friend."

"Apparently."

"I don't know where to start either," I said, my fingers fidgeting with the edge of the tablecloth. "I think we start with honesty."

Josh leaned back in his seat, his expression serious as he nodded. "Okay. Honesty it is."

"Brutal honesty. Even if we think it'll hurt, the truth is what we need to build trust." I held my breath for his answer.

Devon interrupted, holding a pad and pen ready to take our order. Josh ordered a large pizza and mozzarella sticks.

"Maybe we could each take a turn," I suggested. "You go first."

I snapped my fingers to break the tension. "DD, get down."

DD used her nose to flick Josh's hand onto her head when he stopped rubbing. He was so tender as he rubbed behind her ears.

"I loved your mom. Her smile melted my heart. She was fierce and beautiful," he said, his voice dropping to a whisper.

Feeling the weight of his words, I rubbed my hands together. "I've been angry with you for as long as I can remember."

His eyes glowed with heavy sadness. "I'm sorry I didn't protect her." He dropped his head, regret radiating from him like steam in a sauna.

"I know she loved you. I can feel it in the words that she wrote. I blamed you for her death. I thought that if she'd stayed with my father, we could have been a happy family." The bitterness rolled off my tongue, sharp and hostile.

"I've blamed myself every day she's been gone." He took another sip of water and rubbed his forehead as if the weight of his past was too heavy to bear. DD, oblivious, curled up by his feet, sound asleep. "My world fell apart the day your mother was murdered. I haven't been the same since. But seeing you... Seeing you made me realize that she'd be so disappointed in the life I've lived."

"I miss her. I don't even remember her, but I still miss her," I said.

"I miss her, too. A piece of my heart died the day she died." His voice cracked, and I could see the anguish etched on his face.

"I read in my mother's journal that you wanted to adopt me and legally be my father. Is that true?"

He nodded, his gaze unwavering. "True."

"Then why did you just let me go?"

Josh winced at my words. A flash of guilt shown on his face. He shifted in his seat. "We were scared. Catalina was a serious threat. At the time, it was the best idea. None of us expected you'd be gone this long."

Devon set our food onto the table with a stack of plates and napkins. "We received one letter from Gray and then total silence for a year. I scraped together every penny I had and went looking for Catalina. I thought that if I could find her and turn her into the police, you could come home.

"Ten years later, no Catalina, and I was filled with bitterness, hatred, and revenge. I returned to Southport a changed man. I started my business cleaning the boats at the yacht basin and kept to myself. Each day ticked by, and I grew angrier."

"I never once considered how her death made you feel. I was just so angry that I was robbed of a life with my mother."

"I can relate." The corners of his mouth stretched into the tiniest smile, a flicker of connection sparking between us. "Tell me about you. What do you like to do?"

"I like to read. Back in Mon..." I caught myself and paused. "Back home, I have a giant library filled with rows and rows of books. My favorite school subject is math, and I love horses. Well, animals in general."

"Your mom loved books, too. She wanted to be a writer. Did you know that?"

"I didn't know that."

"What do you mean by school subject? What other subjects are there?" He laughed, breaking the tension.

I took a bite of pizza, and it burned the roof of my mouth. Josh passed me a water glass as I fanned my mouth with my hand. I managed to squeak out, "Hot. Hot." I wiped my mouth with a napkin and said, "Gray made sure I learned survival skills, too. Gardening, cooking, knife throwing, hunting, sniper shooting, hand-to-hand combat. You know, the usual things."

"Nothing is usual about that." Josh shook his head, amusement flickering in his eyes. "But, I'm not surprised."

I locked my gaze with his, feeling the gravity of our shared past. "Why do you think he gave me your last name?"

Josh took the final bite of his pizza and shrugged. "Honestly, I have no idea. Your dad and I weren't what you'd call friends." He air-quoted the word friends. "We learned to respect each other because we loved your mother. Gray never tried to hide that fact. He loved your mother just as much as I did, but she chose me."

DD was still sound asleep under the table at Josh's feet. I cleaned my hands with a wet wipe and reached for my bag. Josh asked the waitress to bring our check. I thumbed through my wallet for some cash.

"I've got it," Josh said. "It's my pleasure to treat you to lunch. Maybe we can do it again sometime?"

"I'd like that," I said, surprised by the sincerity in my own voice.

The goodbye was awkward. Josh leaned in for a hug, and I tensed up. He sensed my hesitation and put his arm out to pat my shoulder as I stuck my hand out for a handshake. *Screw it.* I reached my arm around his back and mustered up a short side hug. "Thanks for lunch."

DD and I crossed the street to the ice cream shop. I promised her a pup cup yesterday, but I didn't deliver.

Noah was sitting at a picnic table eating a double-scoop cone that was dripping down the sides. "Hey, Hope," he said, and I couldn't help it when I smiled. His tone sent tingles down my spine. "What are you doing here?" He used the tip of his tongue to lick the ice cream dripping down the side of the cone.

"I promised DD a pup cup?" I kept my eyes trained on the server behind the window. I was afraid if I looked at Noah, I might melt. His black hair was messy, and his throwback Pac-man sweatshirt was precious. "Do you own a shirt from this decade?"

Pretending to be offended, he looked down. "What, you don't like my sweatshirt?" With a mischievous grin, he handed me his ice cream cone. "Hold this." Clenching the hem of his shirt, he pulled it over his head, balled it up, and threw it at me. "Better?"

I think my jaw hit the floor. Trying to seem casual, I blew him off. "I mean. I guess it's better."

Who was I kidding? His bare chest was massively better.

I took the pup cup from the girl at the counter and set it on the ground for DD. She immediately dove in, her tail wagging with excitement.

Noah stood beside me, his presence radiating warmth as he gently brushed the hair off my shoulder. His fingertips grazed my neck, sending an unexpected jolt through me. I swallowed hard and struggled to maintain my composure as he gazed into my eyes with an intensity that made my insides warm. "I'd love to hang out sometime."

Prickles shot down my legs, and my breath quickened. I looked down to avoid answering the question.

"Nothing crazy," he continued, his tone lightening as if sensing my hesitation. "We can do math or read. Maybe play trivia games."

He shivered. The weather had been warmer than normal, but today was seasonably cold. Clearing my throat, I handed him back his sweatshirt and finally managed to push out a few words. "Okay. Sure."

TWENTY FOUR

Hope

Beside herself, Helen hurried into the bookstore and said, "The historical society will be here any minute, and I'm not ready."

I stopped fixing the poinsettia display and walked toward Helen. "How can I help?"

Noah, dressed in a Lego Batman T-shirt and khaki shorts, sauntered over and took the plastic bags from Helen's arms.

Helen said, "Thank you. You both can help me arrange the chairs. We usually turn all the chairs to face the same direction. We can put the chess boards in the storage closet."

Drew appeared with fresh coffee and a tray of Burney's. "Helen, where do you want this?" He nodded at the items in his hands. Helen pointed to the console table in the corner.

Noah and I worked on the chairs while Helen and Drew organized the food and drinks.

"Are you free to get together tonight?" Noah asked.

His question caught me off guard. I felt a flutter of nerves in my stomach, and before I could think, I blurted out, "Maybe tomorrow." I don't know why I said that. I was only hanging out with DD tonight.

His eyes locked onto mine, and the corner of his lips curled into a smirk, teasing but warm. "Tomorrow then."

I smiled. "We'll see."

"Sure, sure," Noah said as he turned the last chair and adjusted it to face the others.

I walked toward the staff room to wash my hands. I could feel Noah following close behind. Standing at the sink, I lathered my hands with soap and washed for several seconds.

Noah tried to sneak up behind me. I sensed his presence, but I played along. In a swift movement, he pressed his hands to the counter on either side of my waist, effectively trapping me. I turned the water off. Barricaded between Noah's arms, the paper towels were out of reach. I turned to face him, and we accidentally head-butted.

"Shit! Ouch," Noah exclaimed. He stepped back with a sheepish grin and rubbed his forehead. I couldn't help but laugh, the sound bubbling up unexpectedly.

"I'm so sorry." I reached for his head to check for bumps or bruising.

Dropping his head in mock defeat, he said. "That's what I get for trying to act cool." His shoulders slumped as if the weight of the world rested on them. He was more adorable every day.

I put my hands on his cheeks, brought his head toward my lips, and kissed his forehead. "Does that help some?" A smile radiated from his lips. His gaze flickered from my eyes to my mouth, and I felt a shiver of anticipation. He leaned in slowly...

But he pulled back, breaking the moment as he said, "We should go. People are arriving."

"Right," I managed to say. *Uggg.* My heart sank; I wanted him to kiss me.

A dozen towns folk had arrived for Helen's historical society meeting. At the front counter, we met Ava, who was setting up refreshments. She looked up, her brow furrowing slightly. Glancing around the room, she said, "The group is smaller today than usual."

"Are your mom and dad coming?" I said.

"They couldn't make it today."

Noah fidgeted with the napkins on the drink and snack table.

Ava pointed toward Noah with her thumb. "What's gotten into him? He seems anxious."

"How should I know," I snapped, the words escaping my mouth before I could rein them in. Frustration bubbled beneath my skin, and I instantly regretted my tone.

"Woah, killer. Settle down. I just asked a question." Ava gave me a confused look and walked off, leaving me with a mix of guilt and embarrassment. *Why couldn't I just act normal?*

Helen started her meeting, and I was intrigued. She informed the crowd about K and K corporate builders. K and K wanted to build high-rise hotels and condos along Bay Street, but the historical society was able to block them. Highrise hotels were built. However, they were built on the outskirts of town. The crowd cheered and clapped with enthusiasm. Helen also told the group that the Christmas Parade was on the meeting schedule with the town council, and the mayor was considering bringing the parade back. The crowd cheered and clapped again. A more prominent man with thick salt and pepper hair broke into a series of whooping noises. I didn't realize the historical society was such a raucous crowd.

"These folks are serious about their town," I said to Ava, who was folding flyers for Santa's workshop. I picked up a stack of paper and joined her.

Ava looked at me briefly and said, "You good now?"

"I'm sorry. I didn't mean to snap."

She smiled. "Yes, they are very serious about their town. Southport is special because of its history and the quaint, small-town feel. These high-dollar city slingers want to come here and turn our sweet little town into a cash cow." Her neck turned red and splotchy. I could tell the town mattered to her. "Southport is what it is because of the people and the charm. It wouldn't be the same if we let big business takeover."

Everything she said made perfect sense. I nodded. "You're right. I'm glad Helen tries to keep the history intact."

"On another note," Ava said as Noah approached the counter. "Are you two coming to dinner tonight for Aunt Renee's famous chili?"

Noah rubbed his tummy. "Heck yeah. I wouldn't miss it." He elbowed me playfully. "Renee's chili is award-winning. She won the chili cook-off fifteen of the last twenty-five years."

"I'll be there," I said.

DD scratched at the apartment door when she heard me insert the key into the lock. "Hi, sweet girl." She wagged her tail and danced around as I entered, her way of begging for attention. "You must be so lonely when I'm gone," I said in a baby voice while I rubbed behind her ears. "Do you want to go to Uncle Randy's?" DD jumped in circles and then sat in front of the door. She smacked the door with her paw every ten seconds until I was ready to leave.

DD bound through the yard straight to Uncle Randy's back door. She barked and tapped the door with her paw until Uncle Randy opened it. "Well, hello, DD. Is Hope with you?" DD wagged her tail so hard that her booty shook.

"Hi, Uncle Randy. DD's super excited to see you."

Noah and Ava were sitting on the couch when I arrived. Noah wore a University of North Carolina Wilmington hat. I hadn't seen him in a hat before, but he looked cute wearing it. "Did you go there?" I said, pointing to his head.

He pulled the hat off, revealing his smooshed head of hair. He looked at the emblem and said, "UNCW. Go Seahawks! I went for two years but didn't finish."

Uncle Randy put his hand on Noah's shoulder and said, "The price of college is outrageous these days. I don't know how anyone can get a degree anymore."

"Seriously," Noah said. "I felt like I was wasting money."

Renee came barging through the front door. "Fresh out of the crockpot! Let's eat."

The chili smelled delicious, and I was happy I didn't have to cook. Renee set the crockpot onto the counter, instructed us to fill our bowls, and sit at the dining room table. The chili, with a side of homemade mac and cheese, was delicious. No one spoke a word while we shoveled our mouths full. Breaking the silence, Uncle Randy leaned back in his chair, patted his belly, and said, "Delicious."

"Normally, we play games after dinner, but we'll take it easy on you. How about we watch a movie? Do you have a favorite movie you like, Hope?"

Uneasy, I dropped my head and said, "I really don't watch many movies. I prefer to read books."

Nodding in agreement, Uncle Randy said, "Too much television can rot your brain, but a little Christmas classic never hurt anyone."

Renee clapped her hands. "Yes, a Christmas movie."

Ava stood up to help Renee clear the table. "How about that vintage Christmas movie? You know, the one with the guy, his wife, and all the family comes to visit? It's a disaster."

Noah looked perplexed. "Do you mean Christmas Vacation?"

Uncle Randy laughed so hard he snorted. "Ren, did you hear that? Christmas Vacation's vintage."

Renee said, "I guess technically it is."

When I returned to my apartment, a white envelope was tied to my doorknob with a beautiful blue bow. The words "TO JANIE WITH LOVE" were beautifully written on the outside of the envelope, illuminated by my porch light.

I opened the door, and DD stormed inside to her water bowl. "Who do you think this is from?" I asked DD. I set my bag on the counter and ripped open the envelope. Inside was a letter, typed on crème stationary paper with blue flowers.

Dear Janie,

It's been too long. My heart has been with you every day. I know we haven't been able to be together, but not a day goes by that I don't think of you. You are my beautiful baby girl, and we can be together again when the time is right. It's dangerous for me, but I'll be with you when I can. I'm proud of you and the woman you've become. I'll see you soon.

Much love, Mom

"What's going on?" I said out loud to DD. "How can this be possible?"

Is it possible? Could my mother be alive? Immense joy filled my body in a way I had never experienced before. I wanted the letter to be true with every ounce of my being. I wanted to rush back to Uncle Randy's and ask what they knew. *Could my family know she was alive and be hiding it from me this entire time? Could my father do that to me? Is my mother alive?*

I sat on the couch with the letter clutched in my hand as I imagined the possibility. After all these years, could I be with my mother again? DD lay beside me and rested her head on my thigh. Her big puppy dog eyes looked up at me. "What is it, girl?"

She grumbled softly and rolled over with her legs splayed out.

I sighed. "I guess you want me to rub your tummy."

My head fell back onto the couch, and I stared at the ceiling.

TWENTY FIVE

Hope

Frantic, I paced the living room. I barely slept. *Did I receive a little from my mother? Could this be real?* "DD, who can I trust?" DD sat on her hind legs and stared up at me. Her eyes were void of emotion. It was almost noon. Noah was coming to pick me up for our hang-out time. I wasn't ready to call it a date.

I was a big old mess. Yesterday, half of my closet ended up in a pile on my bed. Today, I donned a low-cut, short, bright pink dress and tan boots. "What do you think, DD?" I didn't want to look Amish, but I didn't want my outfit to say, "Do me, baby."

DD just stared up at me.

Patting her head, I said, "You're no help.

My breasts weren't large, but they were young and perky. The dress I selected showed the perfect amount of cleavage. There was a little peek-a-booby, but plenty remained to the imagination. I pulled my hair back into a loose braid and applied lip gloss. I was stealing one last glimpse in the mirror when I heard a knock at the door. My heart stopped, and I gasped for air.

"Three, five, seven, eleven..." I recited the prime numbers and calmed down just before opening the door.

To my surprise, Noah was wearing a collared shirt. The blue and white striped button-down accentuated his chest in all the right places. "Hello, gorgeous. I brought you flowers." He held his arm out with a bouquet of red roses. *Woah, what happened to shy Noah?* His cheeks reddened. *Ahhh, there he is.* I smiled inward.

I gestured for him to come inside as I took the flowers to the kitchen. I pulled a vase from under the counter and filled it with water.

"So, this is where you live. It's cute," he said, looking around my apartment. He ran his fingers along the edge of the couch and lingered for a moment before sitting down. "Where do you sleep?"

"Upstairs."

DD jumped and barked at Noah. "Okay, girl. I'll pet you."

"DD, sit," I scolded her. After I finished putting the flowers into the vase, I looked at Noah and said, "Are you ready?"

"For this hang-out with you?" He flashed a grin and reached for the door. "Absolutely."

He escorted me to his golf cart and ushered me to my seat. I buckled myself in and said, "Where are we headed?"

"If I tell you, I'd have to kill you." He laughed. "We're going for a boat ride. Let's call it an afternoon cruise."

When we arrived at the dock a few minutes later, Noah held my hand as we walked to the boat. “Here we are, my lady,” he said, then bowed.

“This is a beautiful boat. How did you...”

Noah pressed a finger to my lips. “I borrowed it for the day. Have a seat. Relax.”

I sat on the edge of the boat and looked out at the water. It was a beautiful afternoon. The air was cool, and I wished I’d brought a sweater. As if reading my mind, Noah walked over with a blanket, two flute glasses, and a bottle of champagne.

He poured champagne into my glass, sat in the captain’s chair, and started the engine. I followed and sat beside him as we drove out into the Intercoastal Water Way. We rode for thirty minutes, skipping along the water until Noah steered us to a private island. He dropped the anchor and poured us both more champagne. “This is my favorite spot,” he said.

“You must bring all the girls here.” I tipped my champagne glass toward him and took a large gulp. The bubbly liquid burned my throat as it went down.

He chuckled softly, a hint of vulnerability in his eyes. “You’re the first.” He leaned back against the wooden railing and said, “My parents own this tiny sliver of land. I come here to be alone. I’ve never brought anyone here. It’s my private paradise.”

“Really? Just me?” I teased, but inside, I felt a flutter.

He met my gaze, and for a moment, the air between us shimmered with unspoken possibilities. “Yeah, just you.” His voice was low and earnest as if he was revealing a secret. "I wanted to share my special place with you. I thought you'd appreciate it like I do."

I couldn't help but smile. "I do. It's wonderful." The thrill of being the one he chose washed over me like the gentle breeze.

He escorted me off the boat and along the beach. Sitting on the sand were two beach chairs, a large blanket, and a cooler. Near a palm grove, a two-top table and chairs were far in the distance.

"Are you hungry?"

My stomach rumbled, and we both laughed. "I guess so."

He picked up the cooler, and I followed him to the table. He pulled out my chair and motioned for me to sit.

Inside the cooler was another bottle of champagne, three kinds of cheese, crackers, and grapes. He set everything on the table and poured me another glass.

I started counting. "Two, three, five, seven."

"Are you counting prime numbers?"

I blushed. "Did I do that out loud?"

"You sure did," he said. His smile lit up the dimming twilight.

"I count primes when I'm nervous. It helps calm me down," I admitted and looked away, for the warmth of his gaze made my heart race.

Noah smiled, and his expression softened. "You're nervous?"

I shivered as the wind swirled past. "Yeah, I guess I am."

"I'm nervous, too."

My shoulders relaxed, and I breathed a sigh of relief. My stomach rumbled again, urging me to eat. I selected a few pieces of cheese and crackers and broke off a bundle of grapes. "I think you're sweet." *Maybe I didn't say that out loud.* Noah's face beamed with excitement like he just hit the lottery. *I definitely said it out loud.*

"I like you, too," Noah said. "I'm sorry. I'm not a smooth talker."

"You're basically the second guy I've ever known, so you're pretty smooth to me." Noah laughed because he thought I was kidding. I didn't correct him.

Pushing back his chair, Noah stood over me and gazed down into my eyes. "You're beautiful, Hope. I was mesmerized the moment I saw you."

That was pretty smooth.

He slid his hands behind my ears and pulled me to his lips. I tensed but immediately melted into him as he pulled me closer. His lips were soft as velvet, igniting a fire within me that I had never felt before. Craving more, I lost myself in his kiss. I wished it could last an eternity.

"Is it okay that I kiss you?" he whispered, his breath warm against my lips.

I bit my lip and nodded.

He reached into his pocket and retrieved a remote. Pointing the remote off in the distance, he pressed a few buttons, and suddenly, the soft strains of music began to fill the space around us, wrapping us in a cocoon of sound. He extended his hand, a silent invitation. "May I?"

He pulled me out of my seat and into his arms as we swayed back and forth to the music. I pulled off my boots and let my toes squish into the sand. For three songs, we danced on the island without a care in the world. Noah spun me out, then drew me back in and dipped me low. I arched and let my head fall back in surrender. As he pulled me back into his embrace, I felt his lips graze my neck, sending delightful tingles racing down my spine.

I gasped. I wanted more, but our intimacy was happening so fast.

Noah kissed me again. My insides burned when his lips touched mine. I needed time and space. I gently pulled away and returned to the safety of my seat at the table, my heart pounding in my chest.

Guzzling my champagne like a refreshing glass of cold water, I glanced at Noah, whose gaze held a mix of confusion and desire. I knew I needed to redirect. "How long do you plan to work at the bookstore?"

"I haven't given it much thought."

He may have just gotten a smidge less attractive. "You don't have any dreams or goals for your future?"

"Yes. Of course, I do. I want to start my own gaming business." He shoved a piece of cheese sandwiched in between two crackers into his mouth. "I want to engineer a new video game. I've been working on the code for about three years, but I'm missing a few elements."

"Tell me about the game." I popped a grape into my mouth.

"You don't want to hear about it. You're just being polite." He waved his hand at me.

"I honestly do. Tell me about it."

"It's called Vortex. You and your team get trapped inside a giant cube. There's only one way out. You have to accomplish all the tasks in a specific order to move on to each phase of the game." His face was oozing with pride.

"Sounds pretty awesome."

He poured more champagne into my glass. "What about you?"

"Right now, I'm focused on being able to live on my own and getting to know the family I just met." I popped another grape in my mouth. "Speaking of, does Ava know we're here?"

Noah looked away for a moment. "No. She doesn't."

"Do you feel like we need to hide our relationship from her?"

Noah grinned from ear to ear. "Our relationship?"

I rolled my eyes. "You know what I mean."

"No. I don't know what you mean. Are we in a relationship? I thought we were just hanging out."

I pursed my lips and scrunched my nose. "Okay. Why don't you want to tell her we're hanging out?"

"She's practically my sister. I didn't feel like answering a bunch of questions I don't have answers to yet. Plus, she's never been here, and I didn't want her to get mad."

I shoveled more cheese and crackers into my mouth and followed it up with a sip of champagne. Pointing at my plate, I said, "This is perfect."

"I'm glad you like it." I caught him taking the slightest glance at the 'V' in my dress. "Would you consider being in a relationship with me?"

I inhaled and choked on my cracker. Coughing like a maniac, I finally spit the cracker out into the sand. *Sexy, Hope. Real sexy.*

Noah took my hand and led me to the beach chairs and blanket on the sand. I laid on my back and propped myself on my elbows. Closing my eyes briefly and trying to ground myself in the moment, I murmured, "I'm not sure you'd want to be in a relationship with me."

Noah sat beside me and leaned forward with his elbows on his knees, his gaze fixed on the water. "Of course, I would," he said softly.

When he turned to look at me, the sun framed him from behind, casting a warm glow around his face. He was kind and handsome as hell.

Electricity shot through my entire body, and before I knew it, I was pulling him closer, his arms wrapping around me as he gently lowered me onto my back. His lips met mine, and the fire blazed again deep inside. He gently kissed my neck and down my chest. I grabbed his face and brought his lips to mine for another kiss.

But something shifted. I gently pushed Noah back, and catching my breath, I said, "I'm sorry. This is... too much. I'm not in control of myself with you. I'm not ready." I wanted to run to the boat and leave him stranded. The other part of me wanted to rip his clothes off and make love to him on the private island. *Get it together, Hope.*

Although I'd had sex before, I wanted to be absolutely certain when I decided to give myself to Noah.

Noah's expression softened, and he nodded, enveloping me in his arms. "I understand. I'm in no rush, Hope. We can just hang out."

I didn't like the feeling of being vulnerable. *Who am I kidding? I don't like any feelings.*

I nestled into Noah's side and rested my head on his chest. He gently played with my hair as the waves washed onto the shore. And in the safety of his arms, as the ocean played its rhythm, I drifted to sleep, feeling—just maybe—at peace.

TWENTY SIX

Montana - Past

Hope

I was twenty-two and a half and ready to figure out life on my own. I entered the barn tonight with one singular goal: to leave a woman ready to take on the world.

The candle flames danced, casting light throughout the barn. Gabe and I walked toward the shadows, where he laid several blankets over a pile of hay. He handed me a bouquet of Oxeye daisies he picked earlier. Gabe pulled one from the bouquet and tucked it behind my ear. He must have come earlier and scattered hundreds along the ground and onto the blankets. The barn was a beautiful sight, and tonight was most definitely the night.

"Hope, you're incredible. You're the most beautiful person I've ever met. Inside and out." He turned to face me and took both of my hands in his. "You've been my best friend since we were kids. I love you."

Warmth spread across my cheeks, and butterflies swirled in my stomach, eager to break free. I stared at him. My lips parted, but nothing came out. I wanted to tell him I loved him too, but my throat was suddenly dry like the Sahara desert.

He slid his thumbs behind my ears, his fingers brushing gently against my cheeks. Gabe pulled me into him. I didn't resist. Desire shot through me like a jolt of electricity. He gently placed his lips on mine and kissed me long and deep.

"I love your dress." He pecked my cheek and then down my neck. He took a deep, slow breath. "I'm not sure I've seen you in a dress before." He spoke in a whisper as he continued to caress my neck gently. "Tell me to stop, and I will." He slid his hands up my thighs, cupped my butt cheeks, and lifted me off the ground. I wrapped my legs around his waist and squeezed his body into mine. He took a few steps toward the bed of blankets and daisies he'd made and set me on my feet.

I raised my arms as he slowly slid his hands up my body and slipped my dress over my head. He tossed my dress to the ground and began kissing every inch of my exposed breasts. All five million nerve endings on my skin were electrified, and I gasped at his touch.

Gabe was the only boy I had known throughout my entire life. It was like destiny had brought us together. Fate gave me exactly what I needed, but deep down, I knew it wouldn't be forever. Gabe would be just for now, just for this moment. He slid his hands inside my pink lace panties, and they dropped to the ground.

I loved Gabe, but I wasn't *in love* with Gabe.

I grabbed the end of Gabe's belt and pulled as hard as I could, releasing the clasp. Startled, he groaned. He looked sexy in his jeans. I threaded my finger into his belt and yanked his pants down to his ankles. Gabe's eyes filled with excitement, and he quickly undressed himself the rest of the way.

I pointed for him to lie on his back and then had sex with my only friend.

Gabe ran his fingers through my hair. "You're a mystery, Hope."

I slowly ran my fingertips across his chest. A smile spread across my face. I had accomplished my goal, I but wasn't prepared for the heartbreak I was about to cause.

He kissed my head. "I love you, Hope. If you let me, I'll make you the happiest girl on the face of the earth. I want you to marry me."

"Marry you?" I didn't mean to sound so harsh, but I was completely caught off guard. I instantly regretted my reaction, but it was too late. A tear slid down my cheek.

Gabe looked crushed. “Wow, the thought of marrying me makes you cry?”

I didn’t know what to do, so I blurted it out, “I’m leaving.”

“What?” He sat up and looked at me. “Did I hear you right? You’re leaving?”

I scrambled to my knees so I could see him eye to eye, but the hurt on his face cut my heart like a knife, and I dropped my gaze to the ground. “Yes.” One word was all I could muster. There were too many feelings fighting inside my body. Feelings I didn’t understand how to express. “But I…”

“I don’t understand.” He grabbed my hand. “I thought we’d live here together forever. I thought you were my soulmate.”

I didn’t know what to say. My body ached from the pain I’d caused him, but the emotions were too thick for me to explain. I ran my fingers through his hair. “I wouldn’t have survived here if it had not been for you.” I wanted to kiss him again. So, I did. “You were my lifeline, but now I need to go.”

Gabe yelled as I walked toward the door. “No. You can’t leave. I don’t want you to go.”

I couldn’t look back.

I had to keep walking.

Gray - Present

"Where is she?" I shouted so loud that I think the other handful of people in the town heard me. "I know you know. I'll beat it out of you if I have to."

Louisa and Gabe gasped synchronously. "You'll do no such thing," Louisa said. "Grayson Stone. You won't dare lay a finger on my boy."

I wouldn't hurt Gabe, but he was the only person that might know where she was. "She's been gone for weeks," I said, much softer now. Fighting back tears, I rubbed my temples and let out a breath.

"I swear, Mr. Stone, she didn't tell me where she was going," Gabe said.

"Let's try another question. Where do you think she would go?" I crossed my arms and paced back and forth as I waited for the answer. Gabe sat in the kitchen chair; his hands folded as they rested on the table. Growing impatient again, I snapped, "I know you think you're betraying her by telling me. But someone out there may be trying to kill her." Gabe ran his fingers through his hair like he was going to rip it out. "Gabe, I know you love her. Help me, help her."

He let out a breath. "My guess would be Southport. For as long as I can remember, she told me stories about her family in

Southport. If I had to guess, I think that's where she'd go." Guilt immediately flooded his eyes.

Gabe confirmed what I already suspected. "You did the right thing, Gabe. Thank you. You're a good friend."

He stood from the table, walked toward the front door, and paused. He turned and asked, "Are you going to go after her?"

"I'm not sure what I'm going to do yet." And I wasn't. Hope was an adult, and I couldn't keep her hidden on the ranch forever. Part of me accepted that she needed her Southport family. I did my best to raise an intelligent and capable woman, but I was Grayson Stone with a heart of stone. She needed to learn to love, but I couldn't shake the feeling that Catalina was out there somewhere.

"Sir?" Gabe cleared his throat. "If you do go, can I go with you?"

"Did Hope ask you to go with her?" He stared at me. "Did she ask you to go with her when she left?"

His shoulders drooped as he said, "No, sir. She didn't ask me to go with her. Like I said, she didn't tell me where she was going."

"Well, Gabe. I think you have your answer."

TWENTY SEVEN

Hope

Ava was behind the front counter, thumbing through her phone. Her purple sweater vest was adorned with silver snowflakes and glimmered in the sunlight that shone through the window.

She set her phone down and looked at me. "You look extra happy today. There's a special glow about you." She waggled her figure back and forth. "Is there a boy in your life?"

I froze and glanced at Noah, who was helping Miss Daily with her cup of hot chocolate. My gaze must have been intense because he suddenly looked up and caught me staring at him.

Once he had finished helping Miss Daily, he sauntered over to the counter. "What's this I hear about a boy?"

I glared at him. "No boy. I'm just in a good mood, I guess."

Ava hopped over the counter to stand in front of me. "I know that look." She winked. "You'll tell me when you're ready."

Wanting to escape the conversation, I hurried to the closet and grabbed the box of chess pieces. I started placing the pieces at each table when Ava said, "You can stop putting those out."

I scrunched my eyebrows together. "Why?"

"Mr. Paul passed away yesterday. We're honoring his memory by having only one table open and using a special chess piece set." She lifted a brown wooden box from behind the counter and handed it to me. "These were found on Black Beard's ship. Helen usually has them locked up in the pirate display. But today, we honor Mr. Paul, our resident chess champion."

I didn't know Mr. Paul very well, but he seemed like a legend around town.

"He was an extraordinary man." Ava pulled a pawn from the box and held it up. "I know he loved his wife dearly. I think he was ready to be with her again."

I carefully set the chess pieces onto the board at the center table. I decorated the chairs with special ribbons, and Noah made a sign that read, "In Honor of Mr. Paul. Play for Paul." He propped it up on an easel, and we stood back and looked at our work.

"Have you read any good books lately?" Noah asked.

"I haven't had time to read anything. Someone's kept me busy." I shot him a look. "I need a good book, though. Do you have any recommendations?"

A crowd slowly began to form. Each person huddled around Mr. Paul's memorial chess table as they took turns playing. Laughter and some tears filled the room.

"I've been into sci-fi lately. I'm reading a book called K Two – Eighteen B. It's about a planet in a newly discovered solar system covered with oceans. Space X has discovered carbon dioxide and methane in its atmosphere, and they believe there to be life on the planet."

His eyes beamed with joy as he spoke. I loved his genuine excitement.

"I'm fascinated by space. My father didn't keep many science fiction books in our library back home, so I've never read one. I've spent many nights looking into outer space and made up stories about what was out there."

He raised an eyebrow. "You have a library. Like in your house?"

Confused, I said, "Yes."

"You do know that most people don't have a library in their house." He smiled and shook his head.

"I guess I didn't know." Changing the subject, I asked, "Do we have this book here at the store?"

"I work here. Of course, we do. I made Ava buy it my first day." He started walking toward the fiction section of the store, and I followed. *Hmmm.* I tilted my head and enjoyed the view of his backside. Noah stopped and put his index finger on the top of the book. He pulled it out and handed it to me. A giant planet, similar to Earth, decorated the front cover with the words 'K Two

– Eighteen B' in red across the center. At the bottom, the author's name, James Noah, was embossed in shiny blue ink.

"Do we get an employee discount?"

Noah smiled. "It's a gift from me to you, but to answer your question. Yes, we do get an employee discount."

I stared into his eyes and genuinely said, "Thank you."

Noah pulled me into him. "I'd love to read it together if you're interested. We could sit by the water and take turns reading a chapter."

"That would be great, Noah." His kindness so entranced me that I didn't notice Ava standing at the end of the aisle.

"Am I interrupting?" She cleared her throat. "Miss Dallenger's here."

I looked at Noah and shrugged.

"She's the owner," he whispered.

Taking care to keep my voice low, I said, "I thought the owner never came to the store."

Noah said, "She doesn't usually."

An older woman in a full-length winter white tweed jacket and high-heeled black boots stood leaning on the front counter. Her gray hair was slicked back into a bun. I assumed she was Miss Dallenger.

Ava tapped her shoulder and said, "Miss Dallenger, this is my cousin Hope. She's our newest hire."

The old woman turned and gave me her hand. "Please, call me Mireille. Miss Dallenger is my mother." The corners of her mouth turned down as she laughed.

I instantly recognized her high cheekbones and sophisticated demeanor. I just hoped she didn't remember DD chewing up her pant leg. I needed this job and didn't want to get fired. "I just came by to pay my respects. Mr. Paul was my neighbor. I don't piddle with such nonsense as chess. I'll be going soon." She removed her pristine winter white gloves from her hands and sat among the chess crowd.

My eyes bugged out of my head as I told Ava and Noah about DD attacking Miss Dallenger in the street.

Ava said, "Surely, she doesn't remember. She didn't seem to recognize you."

Noah laughed. "Just keep her away from DD."

"Not funny," I said and crossed my arms.

Noah jabbed me in the stomach with his elbow, and I couldn't help but laugh. "That's my girl. It was just a joke."

Ava said, "Your girl, eh?"

Noah rubbed his chin with his fingers and said, "Yeah. Didn't you hear we have a reading date at the waterfront?"

I bumped into Josh as I was leaving the bookstore.

"Hello, Hope," he said. "Are you done for the day?"

"Yes. I'm on my way home."

"Mind if I walk with you?"

"Sure."

We walked along Moore Steet in silence. I turned on Caswell Avenue, and Josh followed.

"Your house with the red roof is spectacular. Why don't you live there anymore?"

"That house is unique for sure. It's been in my family for over a century. My father gave it to me when he died." Josh rubbed his forehead. "It's too big and too full of painful memories. I donated it to the historical society."

"I know. My father told me about the house with the red roof. I showed up here searching for your house to find you," I said.

"You came here looking for me?" He sounded shocked and flattered at the same time.

"Yes. I was angry, and I wanted to tell you off." I laughed and punched his arm. "No, seriously, I don't know what I was looking for. I guess a connection to my mother, something, anything to help me make sense of my life."

"You should have been raised here in Southport by your mother," Josh said.

"Probably so, but my father took good care of me." I wiped a strand of hair out of my face. "As I got older, I became curious and wanted to know more about my mother. That's what led me here."

We approached my apartment, and Josh put his arm around me. "I'm glad you're here." I tensed slightly but then relaxed into him.

TWENTY EIGHT

Hope

I melted into the couch and rubbed my aching feet. DD greeted me by licking my face and wagging her tail so frantically that half her body swayed back and forth. I pried myself from the sofa and let her outside. Starving, I popped a frozen pizza in the oven, scooped some dog food, and poured it into DD's bowl.

With the remote in hand, I flipped through the television channels, but every broadcast was filled with the same reality TV garbage. Back in Montana, I rarely watched TV. My father said it would rot my brain. *Screw it.* I turned the TV off and grabbed my new book out of my bag. I was just about to sit on the couch again when someone knocked at my door.

"Hey, Hope. It's Ava," she said from the other side of the door.

I opened the door and smiled. "Come on in. I'm making pizza. You hungry?"

Ava greeted DD with a pat on the head. She looked comfortable in a matching olive-green sweatsuit. "Love the sweatsuit."

Ava smiled, her eyes brightening. "I got this on sale at the Southport Market." She glanced at the stove, her expression shifting to one of concern. "Thanks for the offer, but I ate on the way home from work. Do you have a minute? I want to chat."

I could tell by her tone that this would be a serious conversation.

"Sure. I was about to read. Nothing important."

"Noah is a good guy and a great friend." She shifted her weight. "He really likes you. I don't want to see him get hurt."

"Are you implying I'm going to hurt him?" I was miffed at the notion.

"No. Not at all. I'm just saying... well, I guess I'm asking you to be careful with his heart."

I opened the front door, my expression hardening. "I'm insulted by what you're insinuating."

"Please don't be mad. I love him like a brother," she pleaded, her voice earnest. "I'd be thrilled if you two got together, but if you aren't serious about him, you..."

"You what? You assume I'm a heartbreaker?"

Ava walked through the door and stood on the little concrete pad outside. "I'm sorry. I shouldn't have said anything. You're both adults. I won't bring it up again."

Beep, beep, beep.

"That's my pizza. Thanks for stopping by." I waved as I slammed the door.

How dare she? How could she? I was hurt and angry with her for suggesting that I would hurt Noah. Although, I hadn't fully considered my feelings for him. *Could I love Noah? Do I even know how to love? Shit, maybe Ava's right. Should I back off until I'm sure?* Gabe's face flashed into my head and a wave of guilt washed over me.

"No. DD, I will not back off," I muttered defiantly, steeling myself against the doubt.

My phone buzzed on the nightstand. With my eyes closed, I reached out and felt around for it.

Crash. Bang!

Shit. I'm pretty sure I just knocked a glass of water and my phone onto the floor. I rolled off the bed, dragging my comforter with me. I touched the screen on my phone and opened the text. The words were a blur. I rubbed my eyes and blinked several times until they finally came into focus.

Noah: Good morning. Sunshine emoji

Noah: Wanna meet me at the waterfront for some reading?

I closed my eyes and laid the phone on my chest. I considered his offer as Ava's words ran through my mind. Who did she think she was? Annoyed, I picked up my phone and replied,

I'd love to

Noah: Great. I'll bring coffee. Meet me there in thirty minutes.

I pulled myself off the floor and stumbled into the bathroom. While staring at my reflection in the mirror, I brushed my teeth and cringed at the sight of my hair resembling a rat's nest. There was no way I would get a brush through my mop. I yanked my hair back into a ponytail and put on a hat I purchased last week at one of the shops on Moore Street.

"DD, we're going to the waterfront to read with Noah." Her tail flapping against the floor, she sat poised in front of the door.

I grabbed the book off the coffee table and threw my bag over my shoulder. I opened the door, and DD ran across the lawn. While locking the door, I noticed another letter fastened to the doorknob with the same blue ribbon. I glanced around, hoping I might catch a glimpse of who put it there. My heart did a flip-flop in my chest. I tore into the envelope and yanked out the blue floral paper.

Dear Janie,

We'll see each other soon. Have faith. When the time is right, I'll tell you when and where. We can be together. I promise.

Much Love,

Mom

I pressed the letter to my heart and sighed. The ominous notes were torture. Every day for my entire life, I wanted to be with my mom. *Is she here? Could this be true?* I was so confused. I considered calling my father to tell him about the letters, but he'd be angry with me for leaving. I still wasn't sure whom I could trust in Southport.

"Trust *no one.*" My father's words rang out in my head. No! This was something I needed to figure out for myself. I tucked the letter into my bag.

DD and I walked to the waterfront. When we arrived, Noah was sitting on a bench swing, pushing himself back and forth. "Hi, Noah." DD wrestled her nose under Noah's palm and flipped his hand over her head. "I think she wants you to pet her." I laughed.

"Come here, DD." He beckoned for her to sit beside him. I sat on the other side of the bench and took the book out of my bag.

Noah handed me a steaming cup of hot coffee. "I wasn't sure how you liked it." He gave me a bag of several different flavors of creamer and a variety of sweeteners. "I also brought you a Burney's croissant."

I moaned. "Those things are unbelievably delicious. Thank you."

We spent two hours reading *K Two – Eighteen B*, taking turns with each chapter. Time with Noah was simple and easy. I enjoyed how he wrinkled his nose while attempting to imitate the voice of Velocity, the planet's leader.

He caught me looking at him. "What?"

"Nothing."

"Then why are you looking at me?"

"You're cute." The words slipped from my lips before I realized I'd said them. *He's cute? For crying out loud, Hope. You're such a dork.* He's "after" cute. His looks don't knock you off your feet right away, but spend a little time with him, and he reveals himself as charming, caring, attentive, and undeniably cute. "After" cute is always better. At least, that's what I've read in all my books. And bonus, he has smoking hot abdominals sizzling in your face. Even better, they are entirely unexpected.

Noah flipped the brim of my hat. "You're cute, too." He smiled and wrinkled his nose.

TWENTY NINE

Hope

Bayview Books was slow today. Noah had taken the day off, but I hoped to catch up with him later. I enjoyed reading our book at the waterfront yesterday, but I couldn't get him off my mind.

"I'm hungry. Do you want some lunch?" I asked Ava.

She pressed the end of her pencil to her cheek as she pondered my question. "Yes. A sandwich sounds good."

"Great. I'll order from Sand Witches. I saw a sign yesterday in their window that they deliver now."

I leaned over the counter to see what Ava was doing. She was working on a crossword puzzle from a game book. "Thirteen down is mallet."

Snarling, Ava looked at the question and up at me. "I know it is. My dad's a handyman. I hadn't gotten there yet."

"Excuuuuussseeee me," I teased.

"It's fine. I just don't like anyone messing with my crossword puzzles." She smiled.

Ava and I were back on good terms, but a little tension still lingered.

Today was boring. We'd had three customers total, and since I'd already cleaned everything yesterday, there wasn't much to do. DD was sound asleep behind the front counter and hardly made a peep all day.

Henry delivered our food, and we ate in silence while Ava finished her crossword puzzle.

"All righty. I've cleaned up our mess from lunch. It's almost two. I'm going to head out if that's okay with you?"

She remained engrossed in her puzzle and gave me a casual wave, which I took as approval. I grabbed my bag, stuck my face two inches from hers, and shouted goodbye. Ava jumped and almost fell off her stool. I doubled over laughing. Dazed, DD woke up from the commotion.

"You were in a trance," I said, still laughing.

Pointing her finger at me, she said, "You're crazy."

She hugged me, and I didn't tense up. Embracing hugs from my Southport family became more effortless every day.

"Goodbye for real this time. I'm going to see Josh at the dock. Stop by my apartment when you get off. Maybe we can watch a movie or something tonight?"

"Sounds good," she said.

Moore Street was also quiet today. I guess the entire town was chilling. DD followed close by my side as we walked toward the waterfront and along Bay Street to the yacht basin. As I walked down the dock, I could hear a man yelling, "Piece of shit. Asshole. Idiot. What an idiot." The voice got louder as I approached Josh's boat. Standing with my arms crossed, I tapped my foot, and DD sat on her hind legs, flapping her tail against the dock. Josh had both hands on the metal trash can bolted to the dock. He was dripping with sweat and used all his might to pull the trash can from the dock.

I furrowed my brow. "What are you doing? You do see that is bolted into the dock, right?"

Josh released his grip on the trashcan, looked up at me, and wiped the sweat from his brow. "Hi, Hope. Was I expecting you?"

"No. I thought I would stop by and say hello." Josh immediately leaned back and looked over his shoulder. "I didn't intend to make you uncomfortable. I just..."

Josh shook his head. "You're welcome anytime. I'm the problem. I have made a habit of avoiding people for over a decade. I don't usually have visitors. But you're my daughter." He froze as he uttered the word, as if the gravity of it shocked him. "I mean... you're like my daughter." He flipped his hand back and forth, searching for the right words. "I don't know what you are to me. But you are my wife's daughter, whom I loved dearly and miss daily."

I could hear the genuine pain in his voice, a reflection of grief that cut through the silence like a knife. If my mother were alive, he had no idea how different things might have been. I considered telling him about the letters left on my door, but the words lodged in my throat, and I decided against it. "What's got you so angry?"

"Nothing important. I have a lot of rage inside." He leaned against the dock. "I'm working on letting go of the past and finding peace in the present."

"I can sort of relate. Southport has brought out so many emotions for me. Most of which I don't understand," I said.

"How so?"

"Well, my entire life, logic's been my guide. I seldom allowed emotion to drive me or cloud my judgment. Since arriving in Southport, I feel like I'm nothing but a ball of emotions." I stood beside him and leaned against the dock. DD lay in front of me. I hadn't realized it before, but Josh was much taller than me. He had quite the five o'clock shadow, but I could now see what my mother saw in him. Behind his rough exterior, Josh Miller was a gentle teddy bear. "I feel like I can't think clearly."

Josh put his arm around me. "Southport has a way of turning you inside out, but she'll put you back together again in a way that'll make you better than ever." He squeezed me into him. "Come on, I've got some lemonade on the boat. Let's have a drink."

DD and I followed Josh onto his boat. *I'd never been on a boat this big.* "What kind of boat is this? Do you live here?"

Josh laughed. "This is my houseboat. Yes. I live here."

My eyes were wide with curiosity. I'd only read about houseboats. I'd never actually been on one before. My father had fishing boats on the ranch in Montana, but a houseboat was new to me.

"Did my mother spend time with you on this boat?"

Josh's face became sullen. In a somber tone, he said, "No. Your mom never saw this boat. You asked me about my house? Well, after she was murdered..." He tensed. "I couldn't live in the house anymore. I couldn't bear to be there without her. Every day was a constant reminder that she was gone. That you both were." He took a sip of lemonade and ran his finger along the rim of his glass. "I came out here to stay on my boat. *The Hammer of the Sea*. She was beautiful; your mom and I spent loads of time on that boat. The Hammer brought back too many memories, too, and I sold her. That's when I left to find Catalina."

A tear trickled down my cheek. I wiped it away and took a sip of lemonade. "I miss her."

"I'm sorry, Hope. I'm sorry that you've lived your entire childhood without your mother. I would give my own life so you could have her back."

I believed him when he said he would trade his life if it meant my mother could return.

"She loved you so much. Her journal makes that very clear," I said as I moved to stand beside him.

His pain radiated from his pores, and my heart broke. Josh dropped his head into his hands and began to sob. He shook violently as he wailed.

I touched his shoulder and said, "I understand."

This poor man had lived in sadness and filled his soul with vengeance and anger for decades. Today, he released a small portion of those feelings and began forgiving himself.

Between sobs, he said, "Every day, I think about the life we could have had. I think about her and I raising you, teaching you to build houses, teaching you to drive the boat, teaching you to fish, and watching you grow into an adult." He wiped his tears. "Now, here you are, a grown woman. I want to answer all your questions, but I need baby steps. These conversations are agony for me."

I didn't want to hurt him, but he was one of the few intimate connections I had with my mother. DD put her paws on Josh's leg and nestled her head into his chest. "Hi, DD," Josh said. He rubbed his hand along her back, and DD collapsed her weight on him.

I laughed. "I think she wants to climb in your lap." I clapped my hands. "Come on, girl. Josh has had enough visitors for today. It's time for us to go."

"Thank you, Hope."

"For what?"

"Thank you for coming home. And thank you for stopping by today." He kissed DD on the head.

"And thank you for talking to me about my mother. I can see how hard it is for you. The ball's in your court now. You can find me when you're ready to talk some more."

I couldn't resist giving him a hug, so I tightly wrapped my arms around his waist and squeezed with all my might. He practically gasped in shock at my grip but hugged me back. We stayed in our embrace for what seemed like several seconds. DD stood beside us and lifted her paw to touch Josh's arm.

"I'll be in touch soon," Josh said.

DD and I waved goodbye as we walked down the dock toward the street. A chill ran down my spine as I turned left onto Caswell Avenue—I sensed we were being followed. My pace quickened as my heart raced in tandem with my steps. I could hear the footsteps behind me speeding up to match mine, and then they were gone. *Maybe I was overreacting?*

DD and I continued on our walk home in the crisp air, my heart filled with gratitude as I recalled how far I'd come since my journey here began. Inhaling a deep breath, I smiled and exhaled; I felt genuine happiness.

Suddenly, a man jumped at me from out of nowhere and yelled, "Gotcha!"

In one swift motion, I high-kicked and spun around his shoulders, straddling his neck. Before he even understood what was happening, I arched backward into a handspring, flinging him over my head onto his stomach. I pressed my knee into his back as I twisted his right arm behind him into a hammerlock. If he tried to move, he'd dislocate his shoulder.

"Hope. Hope," the man cried out. "Hope, it's me."

Clearing the rage from my eyes, I recognized the man's backside. "Noah?"

I rolled him over and continued to straddle him. With my hands pressed against his chest, I said, "What the hell are you doing?"

"I saw you walking home and thought we'd get a good laugh if I scared you." His eyes were wide.

"Why on earth would you think that was a good idea?"

DD started to lick his cheek.

"I didn't realize you were the fourth Charlie's Angel. Seriously, Hope. That was badass."

"It's a long story." I climbed off him and reached out my hand to help him up. "You have a bump on your head."

He dusted off his pants as he got to his feet. "Yeah, it kind of slammed into the pavement when you monkey-flipped me to the ground."

I covered my mouth with my hands. "I'm so sorry. I didn't know it was you." I gently inspected his head. "I'm going home. I was planning to text you, but since you're here, do you want to hang out? I think Ava might stop by, too."

DD rubbed her head against Noah's leg. "Hi, DD. Good girl."

"We can put some ice on your head."

Noah stood frozen like a statue and blinked several times. "Are you just going to pretend nothing happened here?"

I pushed past him and walked to the street.

Noah chased after me. "Seriously, you flipped me over your head. You basically kung fu-ed my ass." Noah scratched his head and winced. "Who are you?"

"Look, Noah. You're cute, and I like you. I really like you." DD stopped in the middle of the street and covered her face with her paw.

Noah looked at DD and said, "Exactly, girl. Me too. I'm waiting for the punchline here. Hope knows how to shoot it to you straight."

"What? I'm trying to be honest." I put my hands on my hips. "I like you. Your nerdy facade and washboard abdominals turn me on."

Noah raised an eyebrow and said, "Again, not sure why you're telling me this."

"My father always said, don't rev up the engine unless you're prepared to go for a drive." I put my hands behind my head and stretched my back. "Do you get my drift?"

"And still, I have no idea why you're telling me about engines and cars." Noah rubbed his temples.

"I think I want to take a drive with you someday when the time is right." I watched his reaction closely, hoping for some sign of understanding. *Why am I so awkward about this?*

"Are you saying you like me so much you want to have sex with me?" His brow furrowed, and he tilted his head, a mixture of surprise and curiosity playing across his face. And maybe arousal? DD raised her paw, covered her eyes again, and groaned.

"I'm bad at feelings." I shrugged. Trying to lighten the mood, I said, "Let me try again. When I drop-kicked you, I felt bad. My heart was genuinely sad that I hurt you. I have unexplained feelings for you, and maybe someday we could go for a ride." I rocked back on my heels, raised my eyebrows, and smiled.

Noah's expression softened as he put his arm around me and said, "I'd like to get to know you better, too, and I will most definitely look forward to riding you someday." His eyes bulged out of his head. "I mean taking a ride with you. I left out the 'with'."

I laughed.

Grinning, he rubbed his head. "Now, can we please get some ice for my head?"

THIRTY

Hope

After we got home, I instructed Noah to sit on a kitchen chair. I pulled the bottle of peroxide out of the cabinet and poured some onto a paper towel. I wiggled between his legs and gently dabbed his head to clean the scrape. I blew on the spot and gently kissed his head.

He reached his arms around my back and pulled me against him. Resting his head against my chest, he sighed, and with a muffled voice, he said, "This helps my head feel much better."

I ran my fingers through his black hair and kissed the top of his head again. He pulled away from me and looked up. "So, are you the fourth Charlie's Angel?" Staring up at me with inquisitive eyes, he looked adorable.

I licked my lips and gently pressed them against his. "What if I were?" I teased.

"I won't tell a soul. I swear. You can trust me?"

I laughed. He slid his legs between mine and pulled me into a seated position on top of him. "For real, whatever it is, whoever you are. I don't care. You're secrets safe with me."

His hands, gliding up and down my back, sent tingles down my spine as he planted tender kisses along my neck. When our lips finally connected, the feeling was electric. Our tongues danced to the symphony playing in my head. I rested my head on his shoulder as we embraced.

After a few moments, I said, "I need to get you ice."

Noah moved to the couch and lay with a frozen bag of corn on his head as he flipped through the channels. DD was chowing down on her dinner.

"Are you hungry? I think I'm going to make some pasta."

"Pasta sounds great. I can help."

"Absolutely not. I kung feud your ass, remember? You lay there and rest," I said. "Would you like some wine?"

Noah busted out laughing. "You sure did." He smiled. "I thought we were supposed to act like none of that happened."

"We are, but I had to put it out there. You got beat up by a girl." I lifted the wine bottle and gave it a little shake.

"Yes. I'll have some wine. It'll lessen my bruised ego." Walking toward the kitchen, he said, "Would you feel better if I told you I like you even more now?" He dropped the bag of corn into the sink and put his hand on the small of my back. He took the wine bottle from me and poured two glasses.

"Maybe," I teased.

Startled by a knock at the door, I jumped. "It's Ava. I forgot I told her we could hang out tonight." Noah poured a third wine glass while I let Ava inside.

"Hey, Noah, I didn't know you'd be here."

"Is that okay?" Noah said and handed her the glass.

Ava scrunched her nose and made a silly face, then laughed. "You gave me wine. I guess you can stay."

Hanging out in the kitchen, we laughed and talked as we waited for the water to boil. Our conversation was uncomplicated and fun. I cracked open a can of crushed tomatoes and poured them into the pan. I sprinkled in a few spices, salt, and pepper and gave the mix a good stir.

"Oh my God, I can't believe I forgot to tell you when I got here. The Christmas parade was denied," Ava said, solemnly.

"What a bummer," Noah said.

She raised her finger in the air. "But! They are going to allow parades starting next year. Southport will kick off the New Year with its first parade in years."

I clapped my hands together. "That's awesome. How exciting."

Ava's smile was hard to miss; it spread from ear to ear. "I want the bookstore to have a float. Will you guys help me with that?"

Noah and I said in unison, "Of course, we will."

I added some tomato paste and sauce to the pan and stirred while it simmered. The noodles were on full boil, and dinner was almost ready.

"Who wants to taste test the sauce," I said.

Noah jumped at the chance and was by my side in a flash. I shook the spoon and dabbed his nose with sauce. "Oops. I'm sorry." When I reached for a paper towel to clean his nose, Noah grabbed me around the waist and pressed his lips to mine, smearing sauce all over my face.

Ava scowled. "Gross. Get a room."

Grinning, I said, "Maybe we will."

Noah wiped my face clean. "Don't tempt me."

"I'm glad you're here." I kissed his cheek and wiped his face clean. "Dinner's served."

We inhaled our food. Everyone was starving. "I guess I didn't realize how hungry I was," Ava said. "This is delicious."

Noah patted his belly and said, "Where did you learn to make sauce like that?"

"Back home, my chef Geoffrey taught me. It was part of my education," I said as I poured us each another glass of wine.

Confused, Noah said, "Your chef? Part of your training? Were you studying to be a chef?"

"I have a lot to tell you guys." I did have much to tell them, but I wanted to trust them first. Noah and Ava haven't given me any reason not to trust them. My skeptical upbringing made it difficult. I always questioned everyone and everything around me. If someone betrayed my trust, I don't think I'd recover.

I exhaled a deep breath. "I want to trust you both. Can I count on you to keep my secrets, no matter what?" Neither hesitated and nodded their heads yes. "This is very important to me. You promise?"

Ava wiped her mouth and set her napkin onto her plate, her expression turning serious. "You're scaring me, Hope."

"Do you promise to keep my secrets?" I watched again to gauge their reactions.

Noah nodded and reached for my hand, his grip reassuring.

Ava said, "You're my family. Yes, you can trust me. You can always trust me."

I wasn't very good at beating around the bush. I just came right out with it. "I think my mother's alive."

Ava gasped, her eyes widening. "What? Aunt Lizzie's alive? How can that be?"

"Are you sure?" Noah's brow furrowed in concern.

"I don't have proof if that's what you mean."

"Well, why do you think she's alive," Ava pressed me, curiosity and worry mingling in her voice.

I padded up the steps to my bedroom and returned with the envelopes I'd received. I laid them on the table. "I keep getting these letters."

They each took turns reading the letters. I watched and tried to read the expressions on their faces. Noah bent the paper to his nose and peered at me. His eyes showed sadness.

"Hope, I can't imagine what you must be feeling. How long have you been holding this in," Noah said.

Ava said, "I know how much you miss your mom. I'm sure you want this to be true. But how can you know for sure?"

"I can't, but I feel like it's her. My heart feels it. She's close. I just know it. I can't explain it," I said with the letters clutched in my hands.

"I think we should tell my parents. They'll know what to do," Ava suggested.

I slammed my hand on the table, tearing one of the letters. "That's the exact opposite of what I asked of you. These letters say I'm not supposed to tell anyone. What if she's in danger? I trusted you two to help me sort this out. You promised to keep my secret."

Ava took a deep breath, trying to calm the tension. "Okay, Hope. If you promise not to do anything stupid, I won't say a word," Ava said.

I glanced between them, desperation edging into my voice. "Do you think it could be my mother?"

Ava's face softened, and she reached across the table to take my hand. "Oh, Hope. I'm not sure I can say one way or the other."

Noah shook his head, his face grim as he drained his wine. "I'll say this. If it isn't your mom, this person is pretty fucked up. That's for damn sure."

I leaned back, feeling the weight of uncertainty settle over me. "I don't know what I'm going to do. I guess I'll wait for more letters."

Noah had fallen asleep on the couch. I covered him with a blanket and then turned the television off. Ava stood and stretched. "For such an old movie, Top Gun is still pretty freaking awesome."

"I agree," I whispered. I pointed to Noah on the couch. "I'm trying not to wake sleeping beauty." DD was curled up by his side like two peas in a pod.

I walked out front with Ava. "I'll see you tomorrow at work. It's Santa's Workshop, don't forget." She hugged me. Surprisingly, her embrace was warm and welcomed.

"I'll be there. Elf costume and all," I said.

I went back into the house and slowly closed the door, trying to make as little noise as possible. DD must have heard the door creak, and she started to bark. Noah shot up and looked around. "What? What? I'm up. Is everything ok?"

I laughed. His hair was smooshed to one side and sticking up in several directions. *You're adorable.* "Everything's fine. You fell asleep." I let DD outside to do her business before bed. "You're welcome to stay here. You've had a few glasses of wine and probably shouldn't drive home."

"Yeah. You're probably right. Drunk walking is dangerous." He laughed.

"I forgot you walked. Well, you're welcome to stay anyway," I said and batted my eyelashes.

"I'd love to stay."

He followed me upstairs to my bedroom where DD curled up on the foot of the bed. "I see you have our book on your nightstand."

"Yes, I read some in bed," I said. "How do you sleep?"

"What do you mean?"

"I like to sleep in a tank top and my underwear. Is that okay?" I pulled off my shirt, then my pants.

"Ummm. I... well, uh—you're beautiful," Noah said, then smacked himself in the head. "Shit. Ouch." He hit himself square on his bump.

"Oh no. Your head. Are you okay?"

He nodded slowly. "I don't know why I said that." He smacked his forehead, groaning. "Ugg, not again." He rubbed his temples. "My head is fine. What I'm trying to say is that you're beautiful, but that doesn't answer your question." He fidgeted with his buckle. "I'll sleep however you want me to sleep. I want to make sure you're comfortable."

I turned around, unhooking my bra, and pulled a tank top over my head. Turning back to him, I said, "I want you to be comfortable. Wear whatever you want."

A grin spread across his face as he stripped down to his baggy pair of Grinch Christmas boxers and slid under the covers. I nestled under his arm, and we took turns reading until we fell asleep.

THIRTY ONE

Noah

A rhythmic soft snore, barely audible, escaped from Hope's mouth. She lay tucked under my arm while I stared at her ceiling. *I'm staring at Hope's ceiling.* Of all the days I had to wear my Grinch Boxers, I chose the day that Hope invited me into her bed.

I was afraid to close my eyes and go to sleep, fearing I'd wake up and find out laying next to her was a dream. I wanted to pinch myself to ensure this moment was real. My heart was exploding with joy. From the instant Hope cautiously entered the Museum of Southport, I was drawn to her like a moth to a flame. Everything about her intrigued me. When I was around her, I acted like a ten-year-old boy who saw a beautiful girl for the first time.

Hope rolled onto her other side, facing away from me. I shifted toward her and gently stroked her hair. She smelled like roses on a warm, sunny day first thing in the morning. I couldn't explain my fast feelings. I felt like this girl was meant to be part of my life, as if somehow destiny had brought us together. We might be the only two people on the planet who liked Abstract Algebra. I laughed at myself, and Hope groaned in her sleep.

I put my hands behind my head and stared back up at the ceiling. I couldn't sleep. I found it almost impossible to lie in bed beside this incredible woman and keep my hands off her. She was most definitely the fourth of Charlie's Angels, and I was utterly and totally in love with her. The instant she flung me over her head, pressed her knee into my back, and twisted my arm to the point of dislocation, I knew. I knew she was the woman I not only wanted but needed to spend the rest of my life with.

Hope wasn't like any other girl I'd been with before. She guarded her heart intently and had difficulty expressing her emotions. She was impossible to read, which made me want her even more. She was brilliant and beautiful. Her smile could light up the room, and her laughter was contagious. At the same time, she could kick your ass without even breaking a sweat. *Who is she?* I honestly had no idea, and I didn't care. My heart wanted what it wanted, and it wanted her.

Apparently, something else on my body wanted her, too. I lifted the covers. *Yep, he definitely wanted her.* I slipped out of bed and tip-toed to the stairs. In the kitchen, I poured myself a glass of water and guzzled the liquid like I hadn't drunk anything in days. I wiped my forehead and filled the glass again.

"Noah?" The sleepiest voice whispered from behind me. I turned to find Hope in her underwear and tank top. Her firm breasts, perfectly round, peeked out of the top.

"I couldn't sleep," I said.

She seemed saddened by my statement. "I'm sorry. Were you uncomfortable?"

Realizing she thought I didn't want to be in her bed, I said, "Not at all. I was very comfortable."

She walked past me and opened the fridge. Her ass looked amazing in her purple underwear adorned with a lace edge. Holding a bowl of strawberries, she turned and closed the refrigerator door with her foot.

I moaned.

She turned her head toward me and smirked. "What was that noise for?"

"Truth?"

I took the bowl of strawberries from her hand and set them on the counter. Hope looked confused. I picked her up, wrapped her legs around me, and put her on the counter next to the bowl. I couldn't hold it together anymore. I needed to be with her like I needed oxygen to breathe. My arms caressed her back as our lips locked. I felt dizzy, and my knees were weak. I kissed her again and again, slipping between intense, uncontrollable desire and passion. Her breathing quickened, and she squeezed my ass, pulling me into her.

Finally, I could pry my lips from hers long enough to answer her question. "You're amazing. I had to get out of your bed because I couldn't stop thinking about touching you." Feeling a little calmer, I savored the moment as I kissed her neck and shoulders and slipped the tank top strap down her arm. I gazed into her eyes and said, "I made that noise because I couldn't control my desire anymore."

I wanted to tell her that I loved her. I wanted to tell her that I wanted to spend the rest of my life with her. I wanted her to know I would protect and cherish her for the rest of our lives. But I was afraid. I tried to read her expression to determine my next move, but she was impossible to read as usual.

She slid her hands under the waistband of my Grinch boxers and touched my bare ass cheeks. Passion pumped through my veins. "I want to be with you, Hope," I whispered.

She crossed her ankles behind my back and pulled me into her more. Her lips kissed my face until our mouths found each other. I pulled her tank top down and cupped her perfect breasts in my hand. My tongue danced across her nipple, and she gasped. "I want to be with you, too. Noah."

The sound of my name rolling off her tongue sent my senses into overdrive. I scooped her off the counter, ready to charge up the stairs and make love to her. She put her feet on the floor, slid her hands back into the waistband of my boxers, and let them fall to my ankles. I watched in awe as she pulled her tank top off and slipped out of her purple panties. Her naked body, a perfect specimen, standing before me, highlighted by a sliver of light. I hardened like I've never experienced before.

Neither one of us could wait another second. We rushed toward each other in the kitchen of her apartment and made love for the first time.

For the second time, we took it to the bedroom.

THIRTY TWO

Hope

Noah was sound asleep with the slightest grin on his face. I looked up at him and smiled. I reached over to my night stand, grabbed my mom's journal and opened it to the next entry.

Dear Janie Bug,

Yesterday, I married the man of my dreams. My forever love. Josh is the best man I've ever known, and I am so grateful that we can raise you together. You are a lucky little girl with two dads who love you tremendously. Plus, your aunt and uncle, Helen and Drew, and the rest of the town. Gray and I didn't always see eye to eye, but he wants the best for you and loves you unconditionally. Josh is the father who chose you. He decided to spend the rest of his life with you and me, and yesterday we made it official. I feel like the luckiest woman in the world.

Mom's Words of Wisdom

Don't be afraid to open your heart to love. Being vulnerable, for trusting your heart with someone can be scary. But in the end, it's the most beautiful feeling to love and trust someone completely, to know that there is one person on this earth who sees you for who you are and loves every aspect of you. Someone who will kiss you with morning breath, hold you when you're sick, and ride or die with you no matter what. There may be someone who'll break your heart, but don't let that keep you from finding your one true love. David Viscott said, "To love and be loved is to feel the sun from both sides." You deserve to feel the sun from both sides, Janie Bug. No matter what you do, remember to open your heart to true love.

Love, Mom

Her words hit me hard today. I lay in bed and snuggled against Noah. *Is he my one true love? I don't know. Am I willing to find out? I think so, but I'm not sure.* My mother's words give me the courage to try. I am afraid of love. I don't understand its emotional entanglements. I understand Drake's Equation and Newton's Laws of Physics but don't understand basic human emotion.

However, during my years of extensive reading, I learned that love isn't basic. Love is painful and messy, but for whatever reason, human beings think love is worth all the fuss.

Noah grumbled softly as he slowly opened his eyes. His gaze was fixed on me. "Am I dreaming?"

I propped myself onto my elbow and smiled at him. "Nope. Not dreaming?"

"So, if I kissed you right now, this would be real?"

"Yup," I said.

He rolled on top of me, brushed the hair out of my face, and kissed me—morning breath and all! His kiss was slow and tender, and his touch was kind. A new feeling swirled around my tummy, and my toes curled as he tenderly placed kisses all over my body. When he reemerged from under the covers, he whispered in my ear. "I'm going to rev up your engine, but you're in the driver's seat. We will only take the car for a spin again if you want to."

He disappeared under the covers. I dropped my mother's notebook on the floor and ran my fingers through his hair. If I were capable of love, I thought I might be able to love Noah Whitlock.

Later that afternoon, Noah and I arrived at the bookstore with DD in tow. Inside we spotted Ava, already dressed as a reindeer and setting up for Santa's Workshop.

With my costume in hand, I made my way to the staff room. I glanced back to see DD and Noah trailing behind me. Smirking, I held up a hand. "Ladies only," I said and closed the door in his face.

He gave an exaggerated sigh. "That's so not fair," he called out. "I already saw you naked last night and again this morning." A deep laugh followed, and I could practically see his mischievous grin through the door.

I dug into my bag and pulled out a pair of white tights patterned with festive red stripes, each red band bordered by a thin green line. The green velvet elf dress, trimmed in jagged edges, had a cheerful holiday feel, while a wide black belt with a giant silver buckle wrapped snugly around my waist. To top it off, I fastened a red collar around my neck, each pointy triangle capped off with a jingling bell. After French braiding my hair, I added the final touch—a floppy elf hat, complete with attached pointy ears.

I opened the door to find Noah leaning against the frame, a grin spreading across his face. "It's about time," he teased. "You're the cutest little elf I've ever seen." He tapped the tip of my nose.

I rolled my eyes at him and began to apply makeup while he changed alongside me in the staff room. Rosy red cheeks, gold glitter eyes, and shiny red lips made the perfect elf face. Noah pulled on his yellow tights and green elf jacket. His collar was white and pointed, with jingle bells affixed to each point. His elf hat did not have matching ears, but he looked adorable.

I attached a headband of reindeer antlers to DD's head. Shaking my finger in her face, I said, "Be a good girl today, and you can hang out with us all day."

We helped Ava set up the different stations.

Station number one was reindeer food. Station two, sugar cookie decorating, and station three, ornament making. My mom was brilliant. She invented several stations for the kids to stay busy while they waited to get their picture taken with Santa. As the children arrived, they received a number. Photos with Santa were taken in order by number. While parents and kids waited, they could rotate through the stations, read books, and participate in various activities. Knowing that my mom started this tradition and that, twenty years later, Ava still hosted the event at Bayview Books made me feel like my mom was by my side.

Randy and Renee arrived dressed as Mr. and Mrs. Claus.

"I had no idea you were playing Santa." I patted Uncle Randy on his belly, which had magically become much larger than normal.

"Ho, ho, ho." Randy laughed with both hands on his belly. "We can't have Santa's workshop without Santa."

Renee laughed. "We've been Santa and Mrs. Claus since the first Santa's Workshop. For us, it's a way to honor your mom." She put her things behind the counter. "Helen and Drew will be here, too. We all participate."

I marveled at the room around me. Surrounded by the most incredible people, I beamed with gratitude and smiled. My mother's presence radiated through the joy this event brought. Helen and Drew arrived just as we were putting the final touches on the setup.

Helen was the book fairy. She wore a long dress with covers of children's books all over the fabric. Magnificent, white, sparkly wings adorned her back while a jeweled crown rested upon her head. Her wand, she said, granted book wishes. Drew was the Book Fairy Prince. He held a golden book nestled on top of a small blue satin pillow.

Ava clapped her hands to get everyone's attention. "Okay, everyone—Helen and Drew will be down here by the fireplace reading Christmas stories. Each volunteer will choose a station. Your job at each station is to keep the supplies stocked and help the children." She gestured animatedly around the room, pointing out each station as she spoke. "Noah and Hope, you're upstairs helping to take pictures with Santa. Make sure everyone gets a candy cane when they've finished sitting on Santa's lap. Upstairs is fully decorated like the North Pole. I'll keep things moving and help to serve hot chocolate. Any questions?" She looked around the room. "Okay, places, people. Places." She clapped her hands again. "I'm going to open the door."

I climbed the stairs to get to work and was astonished by the transformation of the space. Ava single-handedly finished decorating the upper floor by herself after I left yesterday afternoon. I had contributed some each day leading up to the event, but I had no idea how much was still to be done. The pirate ship had been creatively transformed into Santa's sleigh. I counted a total of twelve Christmas trees, and assisted with only seven of them. I had no idea there were five more waiting to be assembled.

Noah beamed at me, his eyes sparkling with excitement. "Isn't it fantastic?" He squeezed my hand. "Ava went all out this year. She wanted this event to be extra special because you're here."

Feeling a swell of gratitude and affection, I smiled back. "It's incredible."

Uncle Randy took his seat in Santa's oversized chair. DD lay on the floor beside Santa and rested her head on her paws. The line went on for hours, but I enjoyed every minute. Watching child after child experience the magical joy of the Santa's Workshop event was epic. I was proud to be my mother's daughter and proud of my family who loved her enough to continue the tradition in her honor.

"Ho, ho, ho, what do you want for Christmas, little boy," Uncle Randy said for the four hundredth time. He *never* tired. He was just as boisterous and engaged with the first child as he was with the last.

After several hours, Ava called it a night. Everyone stayed, even the volunteers, to help clean up. She ordered pizza for the group, and we worked until it arrived.

"Pizza's here. Come and eat," Noah said.

Ava climbed onto a chair and said, "This was our biggest turnout yet, with two hundred and ninety-three children coming to visit the Bayview Books Santa." We clapped, cheered, and clinked our paper cups filled with hot chocolate and juice. "Thank you for helping to make this event a success. I appreciate all of you."

Clap, clap, clap.

The sound, echoing from behind the staircase, caught everyone's attention.

"Yes! Thank you for making this year's Santa's Workshop the best ever," the woman said, her voice warm and inviting as she pulled her smooth black gloves from her hands. "I came by to check on the event."

Ava cleared her throat. "Everyone, this is Miss Dallenger, the owner of Bayview Books."

Randy stood and extended his hand. "Randy Levine. It's nice to meet you officially."

Miss Dallenger neatly tucked her gloves inside her Louis Vuitton purse and said, "Ah, yes, Randy. It's been my pleasure watching Ava run the bookstore. I'm honored to carry on the Christmas tradition."

Renee stepped forward, curiosity lighting up her face. "I feel like I know you from somewhere. Have we met before?"

I looked at Mireille Dallenger. Her face was void of expression when she said, "Well, dear. I believe I'm your neighbor. I moved in less than a year ago."

Renee's face flushed, and her neck broke out in red splotches. "I'm embarrassed. I usually know the neighbors. I guess I hadn't introduced myself yet. How rude of me!"

Noah was feeding DD his uneaten pizza crust, and as she chowed down on the last piece, her attention turned to the new person in the room. Suddenly, DD growled viciously, exposing her canine teeth. Noah reached out to rub her head, but she flicked his hand away, growling again in warning.

"DD," I said harshly, snapping my fingers.

"Who let that mutt in here?" Miss Dallenger said.

At the sound of her voice, DD leaped across the table and barked furiously at Mireille. "Get! Get, you filthy—" Mireille shouted, her eyes wide with panic. DD lunged toward her, yelping as Miss Dallenger swiftly kicked DD square in the ribs. "Get that beastly dog out of my store this instant."

Her immaculately slicked-back hair had come undone, with strands flopping around her face. I was lucky Miss Dallenger didn't choke the life out of DD. "I'll take the dog home now. Swing by when you get home," I said, quickly gathering my things. As I turned toward the door, I glanced back at Ava and mouthed, "I'm sorry."

Noah hopped up, his expression serious. "I'll go with you. It's late. You shouldn't walk home alone."

He knew good and well that I didn't need him to take care of me on the way home, but I was thankful for his company, so I didn't mind. Thankfully, DD seemed unphased and trotted along beside us.

Once we reached the door to my apartment, he pulled me into a warm embrace. I nestled my head on his chest, feeling safe and secure in his arms like a cozy blanket wrapped around me. He gently lifted my chin and kissed my lips. "I want to take you to Bald Head Island tomorrow."

I smiled. "I'd love to go to Bald Head Island with you tomorrow."

He kissed me again. "Great. I'll pick you up at eight."

"You could just stay," I said, a playful pout forming on my lips.

He chuckled softly, brushing a strand of hair behind my ear. "I'd love to, but I need to prepare some things for tomorrow. I'll be back in the morning, I promise."

I puffed out my bottom lip and swayed back and forth. "Okay."

THIRTY THREE

Hope

Eager to look great for my day with Noah, I was up early the next morning. After taking a shower and shaving, I slathered myself with lavender lotion. I spent thirty minutes straightening and then curling my hair to manufacture the perfect beach waves. I rifled through my underwear drawer and selected a nice pair of black lace, boy-cut panties and a matching black lace bra. Black leggings topped off with a V-neck white T-shirt and a purple sweater, I decided was the perfect look. I pulled on a pair of light brown, Ugg boots, flipped my head up and down to fluff my hair, and was ready to go.

At precisely eight o'clock, Noah was standing outside my door, holding a mint green harness with silver paw prints and a matching leash for DD. He knocked and walked right in. DD went berserk, her excitement palpable as she recognized the items in Noah's hands. Her entire body shook with excitement as her tail wagged.

"Okay, girl. Settle down." He ran his hands along her fur and down her back to calm her down. He masterfully put the harness on DD and clipped the leash in place.

"I'm not sure who's more excited, me or DD," I said, pulling a sweatshirt over my head.

We piled into Noah's golf cart, and he drove us to the ferry. "Do you have anything to do today?" He looked at me out of the corner of his eye and smirked.

"I don't have any plans other than hanging out with you."

We pulled into the parking lot. Noah drove around for a few minutes until he found a spot. He rolled to a stop, pushed in the brake on the golf cart, and said, "You ready?"

I nodded. "Ready."

Noah grabbed the humongous backpack from the back seat and strapped it on his back. He also pulled a large picnic basket from the golf cart. "Let's go."

I grabbed DD's leash, and we walked toward the launch.

The white, two-story ferry was full of people heading to the island. Noah slid our tickets through the scanner and waited for the light to turn green. We walked onto the boat and found a spot in the back. DD sat quietly between us as we rode the ferry through the Intercoastal Waterway. The wind from the boat ride whipped my hair around, creating a giant mess of tangles. *Glad I spent so much time on my hair this morning.* I ducked inside the interior cabin and quickly French-braided my hair to keep it out of my face.

The ferry pulled to the dock. The crowd filed out down the walkway and onto Bald Head Island. "This way," Noah said and led us down a sandy path. "We're going to the lighthouse first." The air was crisp in the morning but was supposed to be much warmer throughout the day.

I followed along the trail as Noah guided us to the top of the path. A sign in front of the lighthouse said that Old Baldy was the longest-standing lighthouse in North Carolina. This beautiful lighthouse had 108 steps to climb and stood 110 feet tall.

I looked at Noah and said, "Are we climbing the 108 steps to the top of this lighthouse?"

He laughed. "We can if you want, but I planned to drop our stuff off at the cottage." Noah pointed to a sweet little cottage about thirty yards from the lighthouse. "My grandpa is the lightkeeper. He tends to the lighthouse and the museum. He said we could store our things here for the day." According to Noah's grandfather, the government kept the lighthouse as an active light station until it was deactivated in 1935.

"Old Baldy was used as a radio beacon in World War II. In 1988, the historic light was relit but no longer served as an 'official' navigational aid." He shrugged. "Or so my grandpa says."

"Fascinating."

After dropping off our things, we went to the Bald Head Island Conservatory, where our expert guide Ben took us kayaking through the creeks. Noah, DD, and I strapped into the narrow plastic boat and paddled along the creek. The plants and birds were breathtaking. A few droplets of cold water from splashed into the boat.

"What are those?" I asked our guide, Ben, as I pointed to the gorgeous bird only a few feet from our kayak.

He whispered, "The beautiful white bird with the pointy orange beak is an egret."

"Wow. I've never seen one of those before. And the other bird?"

"The other bird is a heron," Ben said.

We paddled further down the creek into the marsh. A group of birds emitted a high-pitched chirping sound while flying in circles above. "Those are osprey."

"Magnificent." We didn't have anything like this in Montana.

After our kayak adventure, Noah scooped up the picnic basket, and we strolled along the beach. The waves crashed into the sand and retreated as the ocean breathed in and out. A peaceful calm filled my soul. Noah stopped in front of a small dune, and spread a blanket across the sand, and beckoned for me to sit.

"Thank you for this day. I haven't been this close to nature since I arrived in Southport," I said.

Noah poured red wine into two plastic, stemless glasses. "I'm just getting started."

He pulled a tray of nuts, strawberries, crackers, and jam from the basket. He even had a dog bowl filled with water for DD and a few dog treats.

"I used to come here as a little boy every summer to visit my grandpa. According to the tales, Blackbeard used to hide out here on the Island."

I laughed. "What other tales does the island have?"

Noah rubbed his chin. "Hmmm. There's the story of Dee Buff Jones. She was a Bald Head police officer who was allegedly murdered. Her case is unsolved. Supposedly, she still lurks around the island at night, searching for clues to capture her killer."

I rubbed my hands together and let out a light laugh. "Okay. Creepy. I'm good with the stories."

Noah wrapped me in his arms. "Aww, are you scared," he said in a childlike voice.

I shot him a dirty look, and he kissed me anyway. As he kissed me, I toppled over onto my back. Noah positioned himself on top of me and wiped a strand of loose hair from my face. "You're beautiful."

I felt a blush creep over me as he pressed his chest against mine, our lips meeting in a heated kiss. He slid his tongue into my mouth, teasing me with every caress, with every kiss, making me want him even more. In a swift motion, he rolled us over, placing me on top. I pressed my hands into his rock-hard chest, my heart racing as his warm brown eyes twinkled in the sunlight. I leaned over and brushed my lips against his, playfully giving him a taste of his own medicine. He groaned, tightening his hold on me as our lips met once more. He inhaled a deep breath as our mouths touched.

Heavy panting in my ear distracted me, and I turned toward the noise. DD was two inches from our faces, her tongue hanging out of her mouth while she drooled and heavily breathed on us. "I guess that's our cue to go."

Noah let out a growl as DD reached out and touched his face with her paw

Noah had planned a day filled with adventure. We walked the M. Kent Mitchell Nature Trail, which provided an almost three-hundred-and-sixty-degree view of the marsh. Signs along the trail taught us about the flora, and we were lucky enough to see a few bolder fiddler crabs come out to investigate. We rented bikes and explored the island. DD, stuffed awkwardly in an extra-large basket hooked to the handlebars, rode on Noah's bike. Afterward, we ate dinner at a local seafood place with a live band.

"This was an incredible day," I said, lacing my fingers between Noah's and resting my head on his shoulder. DD was curled up by Noah's feet, snoring. "Thank you for doing this for me. I'm grateful we had this day together."

He kissed my head. "I'm glad we had this day together, too."

THIRTY FOUR

Hope

It was almost Christmas, and I missed my father. He would dress up as Santa and climb onto the roof. The memory made me giggle out loud. Bayview Books was officially closed for the holidays. I snuggled with DD on the couch and opened my book to read a few chapters, and sighed. “I don’t feel like reading that,” I said to DD. “I’m just not in the mood. It’s my and Noah’s thing.”

I leaned my head on the arm of the couch and stared at the ceiling. “What are we going to do with our free time?”

DD looked at me and wagged her tail. Guilt crept into my heart for having left my father. Christmas was only a few days away, and he had no idea where I was. *He must be worried sick.* I exhaled and rolled onto my side. My mother’s journal was resting on the coffee table. I bit my bottom lip. *Damn it, Hope. You know you want to read it. Just grab the damn thing.*

Dear Janie Bug,

Sometimes, the justice system is silly. Honestly, more often than not, the rules don't make sense. You grew inside my body for nine months, and I fell in love with you more and more each day. You used to kick my tummy when I ate ice cream, and you especially liked to kick me through the night when I was trying to sleep. But your birth certificate said that Catalina Stone was your mother, so they wouldn't give you to me. All of that is behind us now. I officially have custody of you, and you came home with Josh and me, and we can't wait to raise you together. You'll be the luckiest girl in the world with two dads. Josh loves you more than anything on the planet, and you'll learn many wonderful things from him. He's a good man, an honest man. I want to tell you all about him, but I have to get ready for the celebration. We're throwing a party to celebrate our love for you. Love is the theme, and the decorations are all hearts everywhere. Find yourself someone to love and never let him go.

Mom's WOW – Words of Wisdom

Janie Bug, you must always have hope, no matter what you do or how complicated or difficult life gets. Life isn't worth living if you don't have hope. I wish I could tell you that the world will always be kind, but the truth is it will not be kind. The world will teach you many difficult lessons, but if you always have hope, you can overcome anything and find your joy. Remember that you'll find happiness no matter where you are or who you're with. You must open your heart, let happiness in, and hold on to hope. Martin Luther King, Jr said it best, "We must accept finite disappointment, but never lose infinite hope."

Janie, you are what I hoped for. I pinch myself every day to make sure this life is real. I still can't believe I finally have legal custody of you. I'm legally your mom. I'm married to the man of my dreams, and we are going to be a family. Janie, you are my forever hope.

Love, Mom

I sobbed uncontrollably.

This was her final entry. She was full of joy and hope for the future. These were the last words she wrote the day she died. I thought my lungs might collapse as I gasped for air in between sobs. I tugged at my shirt; my chest felt heavy like a giant elephant was sitting on my sternum. It was like my mother died all over again. A profound sense of despair settled in my heart. How could I ache so terribly for someone I barely even remembered?

My phone chimed. The noise was a text from Noah.

Noah: Hi.

Noah: Do you want to hang out?

I looked at his messages. Droplets of tears hit the screen of my phone, and I wiped them away with my shirt. I wanted him to come over. I wanted to feel the warmth inside his arms. *Weird!* I tried to shake off the feelings. The more I cried, the more I longed to hold Noah's hand or rest my head in his lap while he played with my hair.

Me: Yes. I need you. Crying face emoji

Noah: I'm on my way.

He wasn't kidding. He arrived at my door five minutes later.

"Damn. Were you waiting around the corner?"

He smiled and shrugged sheepishly. "Kind of?" He must have caught sight of my splotchy face because his jovial attitude quickly turned serious. He wrapped me in his arms. "What happened?"

I kept my head resting on his shoulder and told him about my mother's journal. I shared thoughts and feelings with him that I'd never shared with anyone. I told him about growing up in Montana, my father, Hinata, my trainer, and I even told him about Gabe. "Every day, I wanted to be good enough for my mother. Every day, I prayed that if I could be good enough, maybe I could see her again."

Noah didn't move. He kept his arms wrapped around me while I poured my heart out.

"I read her final words in her journal tonight. My father told me that she was murdered on the day they celebrated winning custody. Something in me snapped. She called me her hope. I feel like she knew somehow." I started sobbing again.

Noah must have sensed my knees buckle because he held me tighter. He guided me to the couch, scooped me off my feet, and laid me down. He lifted my head and placed it in his lap. Noah didn't say a word as he gently ran his fingers through my hair while I cried.

"Or maybe the letters are truly from her, and she's still alive?" I covered my face with a pillow and screamed. "I'm so confused," I yelled through the pillow.

When I removed the pillow Noah wiped away my tears and said, "Just let it out. It's okay to let it out."

Thirty minutes later, I finally collected myself and sat up. "I want her to be alive so bad, but I don't want to be a fool." Noah put his hand inside of mine. I began pacing the room. "I just keep telling myself this has to be real." I looked at Noah. "It has to be real, right?"

Noah shrugged. "Hope, I don't know. Have you considered what type of person you're dealing with if the letters aren't from your mom?"

His words cut through me like a knife. I didn't want to consider the letters being fake, but he was right. "Maybe you're right, but I don't want to believe that." I flopped onto the couch, dropped my head into my hands, and sobbed. "I just want to see my mom."

He rubbed my back. "I know, and I hope they are real. But why the secrecy? It doesn't make sense."

I wiped my tears. "I don't know. My whole life doesn't make much sense. Who knows why she'd want the secrecy, but if it truly is her, I'm sure she has an excellent reason."

Noah pulled my head back onto his lap and rubbed my head as we sat in silence.

I chewed my lip and looked up at him. "My mother's journal was full of stories of my childhood with her, and she tried to teach me a lesson in each entry." Noah listened intently, his eyes locked on mine, and I loved him for that. *Did I just say I loved him?* "Noah," I began, searching for the right words.

"Yes, Hope?" he encouraged, his voice steady and reassuring. "You can tell me. Whatever it is, I'm here for you."

"I don't love you."

A flicker of confusion flashed across his face, followed by a look of horrible pain.

"No. No. That's not what I mean." I shoved the pillow over my mouth and screamed again. "I suck at this. Just let me get it all out. Then, you can react. Okay?"

Noah nodded and stared at me blankly.

"I don't love you." I raised my finger as if to emphasize my point. "Right now. I don't love you right now. But my mother said it's important to find someone you can love and hold on to them forever, never letting go. I'm not good at emotions, relationships, or even communicating."

"Clearly," Noah said, a hint of humor breaking through his worry. "I'm sorry. Please, continue."

"I want you to be the one I love. I want to hold on to you and never let go. Noah, I think we could love each other forever."

His smile returned. "You're quite something, Hope Miller."

I wrapped my arm around his neck and pulled his face closer to mine. "I'll love you someday." With that, I pressed a soft kiss against his lips.

He whispered in my ear, "I'll love you someday, too."

THIRTY FIVE

Hope

The scent of crispy bacon and freshly baked biscuits filled my apartment. DD was curled beside me, and the tiniest sliver of sunlight peeked through my curtains. I performed a full-body stretch to wake myself up. I was going to throw on some clothes but decided *why bother*. It's my apartment. I climbed down the stairs in my tank top and underwear to find Noah in his boxers, hovering over the electric skillet.

"Good morning," Noah said and kissed me on the cheek.

"It's a good morning, isn't it?" I said and kissed him on the lips.

"I'm making breakfast. What would you like in your omelet?"

Courtesy of Noah, I poured myself a freshly brewed cup of coffee and said, "I'll have cheese and tomatoes. I'll cut up the tomatoes."

"Tomatoes? Weirdo."

I stuck my tongue out at him and flicked him on the butt with the dish towel. "Louisa grew the most delicious vegetables. My father made me eat a vegetable with every meal. Geoffrey would put peppers and tomatoes in my eggs. I didn't like the peppers, but I loved the tomatoes."

Noah shrugged. "I'll give the girl what she wants."

"I enjoy hanging out with you," I said. "What are your plans for today?"

Noah bopped me on the nose and kissed me. "I like hanging out with you, too." He flipped the bacon. "But I need to finish my Christmas shopping."

"Christmas!" I slapped my hand on my head. "It's here already. I know when Christmas is. I just lost track of time."

"You still have today, and some of the stores will be open tomorrow at least part of the day," Noah said.

Back on the ranch, I made Christmas ornaments for everyone each year. It became a tradition, and the ornaments got more elaborate each year.

I finished cutting the tomatoes and slid them into a bowl. "I don't even know what to get. I barely know anyone, but I'll feel like a jerk if I show up Christmas morning empty-handed."

Noah cracked the eggs with one hand, poured some milk, and whisked everything together. I stared at him. *There is more than meets the eye with Noah.* "From what I can tell, they're just thrilled to have you here. I don't think they'll care. You can make them an ornament." He looked up at me. "What? Why are you staring at me?"

"I don't know, mister one-hand egg cracker. Jeez, are you going to culinary school in your free time?"

Noah laughed. "My mother was a baker before she decided to travel the world. She taught me how to crack eggs with one hand. It's not that hard."

DD scratched at the door. "Oh, my goodness, DD girl. I didn't take you outside." I threw on a jacket and a pair of Crocs, opened the door, and DD ran into the yard. Oddly, she lifted her leg when she peed. She must have hung out with some stray male dogs when she was a puppy. She did a few circles around the yard and finally settled on the perfect spot to do her business. As usual, she took off like a shot after and did zoomies around the yard.

Finally, DD trotted to the front door, where another white envelope with a blue ribbon was blowing across the grass. It must have fallen off the doorknob. My heart skipped a beat as I picked the envelope off the ground and tucked it into my jacket pocket. My mind couldn't focus. I wanted to see what the letter said.

Screw it. I snatched the envelope from my pocket and held it in the air.

"I got another letter from my mother."

Noah stopped what he was doing and looked at me. "Well," he flicked his hand at me, "open it."

Sitting on the couch, I tore the envelope open and reached inside. I unfolded the white paper with blue flowers and read the words out loud.

Dear Janie,

The time has come. Things are in motion. Meet me at the bookstore on Christmas Eve at eight o'clock. We can be a family again. Everything will be revealed.

Much Love,
Mom

I crinkled the letter into a ball and threw it against the wall. "This is torture. What should I do? I don't know what to think."

Noah put a beautiful omelet, two strips of bacon, and a biscuit on a plate and placed it onto the kitchen table. "Come eat," he said. Sitting beside me, he put his hand on my shoulder. "I can't imagine what you must be feeling. Are you considering going?"

"I feel like I have to go. How can I not go? What if it's my mother?" I poked around my plate with my fork. Suddenly, I wasn't hungry anymore.

Noah shoveled in a fork full of his omelet without tomatoes and said, "I don't think you should go."

I shot him a sideways glance. "You don't get a say in the matter."

His brow furrowed, and he leaned closer, concern etched across his face. "I'm your boyfriend. I think it's too dangerous. If you're going to be stubborn and go, you at least need to tell someone. Talk to your family. They can help."

"I'll be fine. I can handle myself." I put my fork down and threw my hands in the air. "You're not my boyfriend. You don't get to tell me what to do."

A flash of pain crossed his face, and his eyes clouded. "Okay, Hope. I see."

Shit. I didn't mean to hurt his feelings.

"Please, Hope. Promise me you won't go," he pleaded, his voice softening, desperation creeping in.

"I'll talk to Uncle Randy about it. Good enough for you?" I crossed my arms and pursed my lips. *I'll do no such thing.*

"You're cute when you're mad." Noah smiled, his eyes sparkling as he gave me a flirtatious glance. I didn't like that he could flirt with me and quickly melt away my anger. "Can we talk about the boyfriend thing?"

"Don't flirt with me. I'm mad at you." Despite my words, a smile slipped out—I couldn't help myself.

"Thank you for compromising. It means a lot to me." He pulled me closer, wrapped his arms around me, and kissed the top of my head.

I melted into him. "You're welcome. Boyfriend."

THIRTY SIX

Hope

When I approached the house, Christmas music was blasting through the speakers. I knocked on the back door, and Ava let me in. "Merry Christmas," Aunt Renee shouted as I entered through the backdoor into the kitchen.

"Merry Christmas," I said.

A full spread of appetizers was already prepared on the island. Everything looked delicious. Uncle Randy came through the garage with a large silver tray in his hands. "Hot. Hot," he warned us when he walked by. "Baked Ziti, hot and fresh. Meatballs are in the crockpot."

Aunt Renee put the Ziti in the oven on warm, and then spread a blanket on the couch. "DD, come on, girl. You can lie here."

DD jumped on the sofa, performed no less than fifty circles, and finally settled into a spot. Her slumber didn't last long. Helen and Drew knocked at the door, followed by Josh. Renee instructed everyone to grab a plate and munch on the appetizers.

"We'll play Christmas Carol Pictionary as soon as Noah arrives. After the first round, we'll have dinner and enjoy the real fun games." Aunt Renee placed a pile of index cards with Christmas Carols meticulously written on one side in perfect handwriting.

"Noah?" I whispered to Ava.

"He's always invited. Remember, he was my friend first," she whispered back.

Helen made a plate and sat down at the table. "Hope, your Aunt Renee here," she pointed with her thumb to Renee, "she's the game warden. She's in charge of all the party fun. You don't mess with the game warden. You do as she says. The fun is mandatory."

I wasn't sure whether to laugh or be terrified. Luckily, Noah barged in the front door and distracted me. He removed his coat and handed it to Ava.

"Hi," I said, an awkward smile flashing across my face. I wasn't expecting him. I hadn't told anyone about us yet except Ava. *Was I ready for everyone to know?*

"Hello, everyone," Noah said with a big smile. I looked at him with weary eyes and chewed my lip. "Hope isn't one for words," he continued, giving me a playful nudge. "So, I figure it's best to get it over with." He gave me a reassuring nod as he wrapped an arm around my shoulder. My eyes widened slightly, and I managed a small, tentative smile. "Hope's my girlfriend. We just made it official." Before I could react, he leaned down and kissed me right there, in front of everyone.

I might die. My heart might literally stop beating right here, right now.

I hate affection in general. I hate public displays of affection even more.

He looked at me and winked. "Now, you can relax. Everyone knows."

I slapped his chest and smiled awkwardly at everyone in the room.

Aunt Renee was the first to comment. "How wonderful." She clapped her hands together. "Now, make a plate of snacks and come play."

Uncle Randy shook Noah's hand. "Good for you, young man. I'll kill you if you hurt her." He squeezed his arm and said, "Nah, I'm kidding." Then he mouthed, "Not kidding."

Drew finished making his plate and said, "Randy's bark is worse than his bite. Don't worry about him."

Everyone was seated around the table with their snacks when Aunt Renee said, "Boys versus girls?"

Helen lifted her arm and twirled her hand in the air. "Yeah, baby. You know it."

Drew said, "Ladies first."

Renee pushed the stack of homemade index cards toward Helen. "Okay, Helen. You first. The rules of the game are simple. One person draws clues, while the others guess. The answers are all Christmas carols." She handed Randy the plastic timer. "You tell us when to start. Then flip the timer."

I'd never played this game before, but I did know quite a few Christmas carols. We didn't play many games like this growing up on the ranch. There weren't enough people I guess. We played guess which chicken would lay an egg. Or sometimes, my father would paint squares in the field, and I'd guess where the cow would poop. I laughed quietly at the memory.

Helen took the first card from the stack. She thought for a minute, looked at Randy, and said, "Okay. I'm ready."

With pencil in hand, she drew two straight, upright lines, then sketched an umbrella shape over them, adding a few circles. The image started to look like a palm tree. I bounced in my seat, slapping my hand on the table. "Ooh, ooh! Mele! Mele Kalikimaka!"

Helen flipped the card to show everyone that I was right.

Uncle Randy blurted out, "Bullshit. I call bullshit." He pointed at Helen's drawing. "Somehow, you cheated. You couldn't have figured that out from this drawing. No way."

Aunt Renee moved the cards to Drew. "Okay, okay. We won fair and square. It's your turn."

This went on for another hour. Eventually, the girls won, of course. It was seven-thirty, and I needed to get going. I reached for my stomach and said, "I don't feel so great all of a sudden." Noah glared at me. "I'm going to lie down. I hope that's okay."

Aunt Renee put some cookies onto a plate for me. "Of course, it's okay. Get some rest. Take a plate of cookies." DD was fast asleep on the couch. "She can stay here. You'll be back in the morning. It's fine."

"Thank you. See you guys later."

Noah followed me out the back door and to my apartment. "You better not be doing what I think you're doing." He grabbed my wrist and almost knocked the plate of cookies out of my hand.

"I truly don't feel good, Noah. I need to lie down." My voice softened. I hoped he'd take the hint.

"I can come inside and make you chicken noodle soup or rub your head."

I shook my head and gave him a small smile. "I'm good. Go, enjoy the party. I'm going straight upstairs to bed."

White, red, and green twinkle lights were aglow along Moore Street. I arrived at the bookstore promptly at eight o'clock. My heart was racing. I could practically hear it pounding on my ribcage. Could this be real? Will I meet my mother tonight?

The interior lights were on, and the door was unlocked. Confused, I scratched my head as I entered.

"Hello," I called out.

"Hope. It's great to see you," a woman's voice said.

The pit in my stomach was ravenous like it might eat my insides. Behind the counter stood Miss Dallenger. I blew out the breath I had been holding since I walked in. *Great. Mireille Dallenger is here. What am I going to do when my mother gets here?*

"I'm glad you came. Come sit," she said. *She's glad I came?* She motioned for me to take a seat on one of the couches. "We have much to discuss."

Reluctantly, I sat.

"I'm sure you have many questions. I'll answer everything, but first, let me explain."

I looked at her with a blank stare. *Could she be my mother?* I searched her eyes for any ounce of recognition.

Her eyes softened, misting slightly as she spoke. "I've thought about this moment every day since the day I lost you." She glanced down, her hands twisting together nervously before she met my gaze again. "I'm sorry that you had to grow up without me. That must have been... difficult."

I swallowed, feeling a lump form in my throat.

"You need to know that I wanted to come and get you." Her voice cracked, and she cleared her throat to compose herself. "I even tried several times, but it wasn't safe. Your father had people searching for me." She looked away briefly, her jaw tightening, before she looked at me again. "Even now, as an adult, you need your mother. I'd like the opportunity to build a relationship with you."

"I don't understand. Where have you been? Why did you leave?" I said as I choked back tears.

"I've been all over." She paused, glancing away, a flicker of something unreadable in her eyes. "At first, I was looking for you, but your father had endless resources. He made it impossible for you to be found." Her gaze darted down, and she gave a quick, tight smile. "When Helen listed the bookstore for sale, I saw the opportunity to hide in plain sight. I bought Bayview Books and moved back to Southport. Mostly, I kept to myself and waited. I was confident you'd return. Honestly, you came back much sooner than I expected."

My head was spinning like a top. I thought it might pop off my shoulders. I had desperately wanted to have my mother back, but now that I was sitting face-to-face with her, something didn't feel right. I was *angry*.

"That explains where you were, but why did you leave? You're right. I grew up without a mother. I wished for you every day, but you weren't there. Why?" I rubbed my hands together, crossed my ankles, and looked away to keep from breaking down. *I've cried more in Southport than I ever have in my life.*

"My life was in danger. I didn't have a choice. I was almost killed, and they were never going to stop coming after me." Tears rolled down her cheek. "I didn't want to leave you, Sophie."

"Sophie?" I cocked my head back as I repeated the name.

"Yes. You're my beautiful, exquisite Sophie Stone. Your father changed your name to Hope when he took you away, but your given name was Sophie Stone."

Suddenly, it all clicked.

I was having a conversation with my mother's *murderer*.

I was a naïve little girl, who wanted to believe so badly that her mother was alive. I'd let emotions instead of logic be my guide. Stupid!

Rage bubbled up from deep within, molten and unstoppable, scorching every rational thought. My vision blurred, the world bleeding into crimson as fury seized me. For a heartbeat, I felt nothing, like I'd slipped out of time itself. Slowly, my sight returned, sharpening back onto Mireille Dallenger—Catalina Stone.

I had trusted her, believed her lies.

The betrayal tore through me. Each thought sharper than the last. I tightened my fists, knuckles white, and through clenched teeth, hissed, "You're even more unhinged than I ever imagined."

THIRTY SEVEN

Gray

An animated Santa Claus on the porch startled me as he came to life and sang, "Ho, ho, ho, Merry Christmas." I knocked three times and waited. Randy looked out the window to see who it was. I smiled and waved. My security detail flanked me on either side.

He opened the door and said, "Hi, Gray. It's good to see you. Merry Christmas."

"Hello, Randy," I said as I walked through the door. With a glance, I told my guards to stay on the porch. "Is Hope here?"

Everyone looked flummoxed by my arrival.

Helen stood and said, "Well, it's about damn time we heard from you."

Suddenly, the entire room was moving in slow motion, and I started to sway in circles. Randy grabbed my arm and guided me to the couch to sit down. Renee handed me a glass of water. "Are you okay?" she said.

Helen sat across from me. "Damn. I didn't mean to send you into cardiac arrest."

"I'm dying. I have lung cancer, and the doctors have done everything they can. Hope doesn't know. She ran away before I could tell her."

Helen sat up straight. Her voice was stern. "We haven't heard from you in years. Why show up now when you're dying?"

I took a sip of water. I wanted to dump the entire glass on my head. "None of that matters right now. Where's Hope?"

A voice came from the kitchen table and said, "She went home. She didn't feel good."

I blinked and rubbed my eyes. Performing quick math in my head, I worked out who the voice must belong to. "Ava?"

"The one and only. It's nice to meet you, Gray."

I turned to Helen. "You didn't get my letter?"

She huffed. "You're joking, right?"

"Not joking. I sent a letter when Hope left. I told you about my cancer and that I was coming to Southport. I explained everything, but I had to get some things in order before I could come because I'm dying."

A knock at the door interrupted the conversation. "Mr. and Mrs. Levine," the guard said from behind the door. "There's a man named Josh Miller out here. I've checked his identification. He says you're expecting him."

"For heaven's sake," Renee said as she stomped off to open the door. "He was just returning from grabbing something from his boat."

I stood slowly and said, "I need to check on Hope." The room began to go dark, and I fell back onto the couch. My guards rushed toward me.

"Mr. Stone, you need to take it easy. The trip has worn you out. The doctor told you this would be taxing. You need rest," Hinata said.

"What's going on?" I recognized the voice even after twenty years.

"Hello, Josh."

"I'll go check on Hope," a random boy said, dashing out of the house before I could even ask who he was.

"Who's he?" I asked, pointing toward the back door.

Ava replied, "He's Hope's boyfriend, Noah. He works at the bookstore with us."

"I'll deal with the boyfriend later." I scratched my head. "I don't understand. Where would the letters go? I sent them to the bookstore."

Helen chimed in, "I'm not at the bookstore anymore. I sold it."

"You did what?" I shouted.

"I sold it. You stopped sending letters. I was getting old." She shook her finger in my face. "Don't blame this on me."

The boy came back into the house. His breath was loud and heavy. "Hope's gone. She's not here."

Renee gasped as Randy said, "Are you sure? Maybe you didn't see her."

"Umm, no disrespect, Mr. Levine, but the place isn't that big. I'm sure."

Ava turned pale. Something seemed to be bothering her so I asked, "Ava? What is it?"

She glanced at Noah, her expression tense.

"Noah? If you two know something, now's not the time to hide it." A coughing fit kicked in, and I gasped for air.

Noah stepped forward, his face serious. "Hope's been getting letters from someone claiming to be her mom."

Josh immediately bolted toward the door. "It's her. I know it's her."

"Wait," Noah called out. "I think I know where Hope went."

Josh turned and impatiently tapped his toe as he waited for Noah to speak again.

"The last letter said to meet her tonight at the bookstore. Hope promised me she wouldn't go." He ran a hand through his hair, the anxiety evident in his every movement. "I didn't think she'd go."

Josh threw open the door. Hinata helped me onto the porch. "Take my guards and my gun," I instructed, my voice firm despite the dizziness washing over me.

Without a second thought, Randy darted past me, calling after Josh. "You're not going without me."

Randy, Josh, Hinata, and Billy jumped into Billy's SUV. The engine roared to life as they peeled out of the driveway, sending gravel flying and kicking up clouds of dust. On the porch, Renee paced back and forth, her hands folded tightly across her chest, her worry palpable.

Meanwhile, Ava and Noah stood in the doorway, their expressions filled with concern.

THIRTY EIGHT

Hope

My heart was racing. I had never experienced anger like this before. "Did you think I would fall for this?" Spittle flew out of my mouth as I spoke.

Catalina was as steady as a rock. She didn't even flinch. "I'm your mother, Sophie. I can't imagine what poison they've fed you all these years, but I am your mother."

"You're completely certifiable." My eyes widened in disbelief as I shook my head.. "You've lost all sense of reality."

Catalina's tone shifted. She spoke with more intensity and intention. "Your father sent me a letter. He's dying. You'll have no one. I'm the only family you have left."

Unable to listen to any more of her gibberish, I stood. "You're full of lies. I won't be manipulated by your bullshit." I turned to leave.

Catalina yanked my hair and shoved me back onto the couch as she screamed, “You don’t walk away from me, you little shit.” Her eyes were black as coal.

Adrenaline pumped through my veins like pistons in a combustion engine. I thought I might turn into the Incredible Hulk, green skin and all. She wrapped her hands around my neck and began to squeeze the life out of me. “You’ll be my daughter, or you’ll die like your mother.” She pressed down harder, and I could feel my windpipe crushing under her grip.

Pushing my arms and hands downward, I rotated my hips and shoulders inward to create leverage and escape her grasp like Hinata taught me. I sprinted toward the door, but Catalina was right behind me. A cold, metal object swept my legs out from under me, and I crashed onto my back.

“Ugg.” I grunted when the wind flew out of my chest.

I rolled backward onto my shoulders, using the momentum to flip onto my feet in one fluid motion. “I’m done being nice.” My foot connected with her jaw in a swift, precise wheel kick. Catalina screamed in pain as she hit the floor, her eyes wide with shock.

With her hand on her cheek, she whimpered, “Sophie. Please, my Sophie. Come back to me.”

I stood over her, breathing heavily, my heart pounding with rage. “My mother said, **Call. Her. Janie**,“ I declared, each word punctuated with intensity. “I’m keeping Janie. My name is Janie Miller Levine.”

Crack.

The room went blurry, and a warm liquid trickled down my face. Instantly, my head was pounding. My vision blurred then cleared and blurred again. I could hear Hinata in my head. *Find your center, Hope. Stay focused. Close your eyes and listen to the world around you.*

Woosh.

Catalina swung the metal object toward my head again, but I was ready this time. In a flash, I seized the rod mid-swing, stopping her blow inches from my face. I yanked the metal object, which I now recognized was the fire poker, from her grasp, spun it around my head, and pointed it at her throat. I was one second away from ramming the poker into her neck, but I stopped myself.

"Ahhh," I screamed in pure agony. "You deserve to die." I pressed the tip of the fire poker against her skin—every fiber of my being wanted to beat her to a pulp. "Ahhh!" I screamed again. "Despite the fact that you murdered my mother, she'd want me to forgive you." I relaxed and lowered the fire poker to my side. "Lizzie Levine saved your life today. Choke on that, bitch!"

"She wouldn't want *me* to forgive you," a deep voice said from behind me.

Bang. Bang. Bang.

THIRTY NINE

Josh

Billy whipped the SUV out of the driveway and raced toward the bookstore. Fidgeting in the front seat, Randy hopped up and down in his chair, as if adrenaline was over-flowing from his pores. Hinata sat in the back seat next to me. His hands rested on his knees, and his eyes were closed.

I checked the clip in Gray's gun. *Full clip.* Perfect. I need only one.

Oddly, I was calm. Randy looked over his shoulder. "Do you think it's really her?"

Hinata opened his eyes and looked at me.

"I hope it is her," I growled. I slammed the clip back into the gun. "I've dreamed about this day for twenty years."

Hinata nodded at me.

"Catalina took everything from me. I spent ten years of my life tracking her all over the country, but I was always two steps behind." I pointed the gun out the window. "Yes. I hope it's her."

Hinata reached over, placed his hand on my arm, and gently pushed my arm back into my lap. "You should never point a loaded gun when you don't intend to shoot it." I looked at him. He was an interesting guy, under different circumstances, I might have wanted to hang out with him.

"Hope's a smart girl. She's tough. She'll be okay," Hinata said.

Randy turned around. "You know her?"

"I was her teacher."

I shook my head and laughed. "You were her teacher?" I pointed at Hinata. "What did you teach her?"

"I taught her to protect herself. That's how I know she'll be okay."

Billy slammed the brakes, and the SUV lurched to a stop in front of the bookstore. The lights inside illuminated the street. I jumped out of the backseat and sprinted toward the door. My heart skipped a beat as I considered what I might walk into. I took a humongous breath and pulled open the door. To my surprise, Hope was standing over a woman holding a fire poker to her neck.

Initially, I didn't recognize Catalina; her hair was gray, and she'd clearly had plastic surgery. But when I looked into her eyes, I saw the heartless, batshit crazy bitch inside.

"Ahhh!" Hope screamed.

Several emotions surged through me. I was proud of Hope, and I knew Lizzie would be proud of her, too. At the same time, I didn't want her life to be marred by being a killer. I wanted to rush to her side and save her. I was also filled with blind rage and didn't care how Catalina died. She just needed to die.

With the fire poker still pressed into Catalina's throat, Hope said, "Despite the fact that you murdered my mother, she'd want me to forgive you." She relaxed and lowered the fire poker to her side. "Lizzie Levine saved your life today. Choke on that, bitch!"

In what seemed like one giant step, I moved beside Hope. "She wouldn't want *me* to forgive you."

I fired three rounds directly into Catalina's chest.

Startled, Hope instinctively covered her ears and ducked for cover as the deafening sound reverberated through the room. She collapsed into Hinata, who had just entered the room with Billy and Randy. She looked up at him. "Hinata?"

Her eyes dropped to the floor and caught a glimpse of Catalina's lifeless body sprawled on the hardwood, a dark pool of blood spreading beneath her. Reality crashed over her face like a wave. I saw sweat break out across her forehead.

Leaning over Catalina, I pressed my fingers to her neck to check for a pulse.

Hope looked up at Hinata. "What's going on?"

"She's dead," Hinata said softly.

"Hope, you okay?" I asked, glancing back at Hope, worry etched across her face.

"I'm okay," she said.

"You three need to go," Hinata said. "We'll take care of this. You need to leave before the police arrive." Billy re-entered the bookstore with industrial cleaning supplies and took my gun.

"Heeeeyyyyy. I recognize you." Hope pointed at Billy. "You were following me." She looked back at Hinata. "Hin, he's been following me, and I beat his ass."

Billy waved and said, "In the flesh. You have a nasty throat chop, young lady."

Hinata smiled. "He was working for your father."

Hope scoffed. "Looks like he still needs some training."

Hinata snorted.

I took her hand. "Hope, we need to go. Now."

"Janie's Hope. Please, call me Janie."

FORTY

Janie

Back at Uncle Randy's, Noah held my hand while Drew patched my head. His carpentry skills extended to medical aid. Who knew? Josh told everyone what happened at the bookstore, but most importantly, that Catalina was dead.

Helen said, "Do we have legit confirmation the batshit crazy bitch is dead? Like no pulse, out for good, dead, dead?"

My father looked frail. I felt terrible about leaving him when I did, but I was also angry that he didn't tell me he was sick.

He said, "Hinata and Billy, my security guards have confirmed. She's dead. Dead, dead."

Renee blew out a loud sigh of relief. "I can't believe it's finally over. She's gone."

Randy wrapped his arms around her. "We've waited decades for this peace in our family." He kissed her lips, and they hugged for a moment.

Josh raised his hand. "Um, I hate to break up the celebrations, but I did commit murder tonight. I'm not sure how that's going to work out."

"Did it feel amazing to squeeze the trigger and shoot the life out of that bitch?" Helen asked, a wild gleam in her eyes.

Renee smacked her in the arm. "Helen!"

Helen scoffed. "What? It's a legitimate question." Everyone laughed.

My father shifted on the couch. "Hinata and Billy are taking care of everything. Catalina Stone was in the wind. Mireille Dallenger was mostly off the grid. I don't think we have anything to worry about."

"That's easy for you to say. You have an alibi," Josh said as he massaged his temples.

My father raised his hand to quiet the room. "Actually, Josh, you have the alibi. And you used my gun. I'm prepared to take the blame. The husband is always the prime suspect. I'm dying anyway, so what difference does it make." My father laid his back against the couch. "My gun, my fingerprints, my ex-wife. You've got nothing to worry about."

"Your fingerprints?" Josh said.

"Yes. My guys cleaned the weapon and hid it, but not before they planted my fingerprints on it. So even if they go looking after I'm dead, they'll pin it on me. You're safe. Everyone's safe."

Helen looked at me and then at my father and asked, "Will you both be staying in Southport?"

My father nodded slowly. "I can't speak for Hope..."

I interrupted him. "It's Janie now, if that's okay with you."

His smile widened, a soft light in his eyes. "I can't speak for Janie, but the trip here was hard enough. Looks like you're stuck with me." As he looked at me, I felt a wave of warmth wash over me, as if he were wrapping me in an embrace. "Southport feels like home. Now that you're safe, there's no place I'd rather be."

My face lit up like a Christmas Tree. "It feels like home for me, too." I sat down next to my father.

He put his arm around me and said, "I've relocated the tenants in my condo and already had a crew renovating the place for the past few weeks. I plan to stay there, and you're welcome to stay with me if you'd like."

Josh cleared his throat. "Do you need help? You know, like help with your care?"

My father said, "Yes, but I'll figure that out. I'm not worried about it."

"Janie and I can help," Josh said as he nodded in my direction. "It's the least I can do for you. You're taking the blame on the forthcoming murder charge."

"Let's not get carried away. Taking the blame is the backup plan; I don't like you that much," Gray chuckled. "Janie, do you want to live with your two dads?"

I tilted my head and contemplated the question. "I guess living with my two dads would be okay with me."

Renee squealed with glee. "Oh my goodness! Look out the window." She rested her head on Randy's shoulder. "It's snowing."

Drew said, "It's snowing. In Southport?"

Everyone rushed to the front porch to take in the sight, but I stayed with my dad and put my hand in his. "Why didn't you tell me?"

"I didn't want to worry you." Sadness clouded his eyes. "You'd already lost so much. I didn't want to tell you that you were going to lose me, too."

He pulled me in closer. "Josh is an excellent man. Your family here is incredible. This is where you belong." He kissed the top of my head. "Let these people in your life, Janie. You can trust them."

"I can see why you and Mom loved this place so much. Southport really does change people," I said as I rested my head on his chest. "I love you, Dad."

"Dad? I like the sound of that."

Grinning, I said, "In Southport, you're Dad."

My dad lifted my chin so he could look at my face. "I have some difficult things to discuss with you."

"More difficult things than you dying?"

He laughed. "Along those lines. I've sold my businesses. I've put all the funds from the sale in a fund for you. You won't have to worry about a thing for the rest of your life. You deserve at least that for everything you've been through."

I sat up straight and furrowed my brow. "Dad, you're not even gone yet. Why…"

He pressed his hand to my lips. "I want everything handled so you don't have to worry about a thing when I'm gone. I've put the Montana ranch in your name. It belongs to you now. You'll need to check on things occasionally, but you don't have to live there. Louisa and Donte will tend to everything. Automatic weekly payments are arranged to go to them and the rest of the staff."

A tear slid down my cheek. I sniffled and threw my arms around my dad. "There's no chance you'll beat this cancer?"

His voice cracked as he whispered, "No chance." He wiped a tear from my cheek. "Trust me, baby girl, I've tried everything." He exhaled a breath. "I've ensured you'll be set for the rest of your life."

I lifted one brow and asked, "How set are we talking about here?"

He pulled me in again and put his lips to my ear. Quietly, he said, "Billions. Billions and billions. I trust my smart girl will spend it wisely."

I hugged him again. "I'd rather have you and Mom." And that's when I broke down and cried in his arms, hugging him tighter and longer than ever before.

Rubbing my eyes, I reached for his hand. "Let's go look at the snow."

I helped him to the door, and we stepped out onto the front porch, the crisp air wrapping around us.

Renee began to sing Frosty the Snowman, her voice bright and cheerful. One by one, we joined in like a middle school choir, laughter bubbling up as we sang off-key but with full hearts.

As we continued with a chorus of Christmas Carols, the snow began to fall gently around us, transforming the world into a winter wonderland. Each flake danced in the glow of the porch light, creating a magical backdrop for our impromptu concert.

I realized that this night was my favorite Christmas Eve to date.

FORTY ONE

Janie

Men in Scottish kilts played bagpipes while they marched down the street. Tens of thousands of people came from all over the country to see the Southport New Year's Parade. DD sat, wagging her tail, and watched as the women in fancy dresses strutted by. Each lady was dressed in a blue gown with an enormous hoop skirt. Beads, rhinestones, and sequins made exquisite patterns along the corset and skirt of the dresses. Blue, green, and white feather plum headdresses covered their heads. Each lady smiled and waved as they passed by.

My father was seated in a wheelchair that we pushed to the edge of the curb. He clapped and smiled as the local high school marching band played *Eye of the Tiger* by Survivor. Helen, Drew, Randy, and Renee were in the parade. Noah and Ava stood on either side of me. We grooved back and forth while we watched the parade go by.

Off in the distance, we could see the golf carts ready to make their appearance. Like a kid in a candy store, Randy beamed with excitement so he could spray silly string into the crowd. The historical society rode in the golf carts, each decorated in a different decade. Helen and Drew were in the nineteen-seventies. Their cart was airbrushed with hearts, flowers, and tie-dye galore. Fluorescent-colored lights flashed from the rooftop, and Queen blared from their stereo speaker.

Renee and Randy were decked out in the nineteen-eighties. Renee's hair was teased so high it touched the roof of the golf cart. She wore a pink leotard with blue spandex pants and white leggings. "Oh my God, do you see this," I said to Ava and laughed.

Josh had just arrived and found us in the crowd. He said, "Look at your uncle," and pointed toward the road. Uncle Randy was dressed like an eighties punk rocker, with a full wig. More golf carts passed by, representing a millennia of decades. One even repped the future year twenty-five hundred. That golf cart was covered in tin foil, with rocket jets on the back, giving it the appearance of hovering over the road instead of riding on wheels.

Surrounded by joy, I looked around and smiled. I sat beside DD on the sidewalk, and she laid her head on my lap. As I pet her head and her ears, contentment flooded my heart. For the first time ever, I was exactly where I was supposed to be. My mother was everywhere in Southport, and I had both dads and a boatload of new family. I didn't know how safe and wonderful a family could make you feel.

I also had Noah. My heart grew fonder of him as each day passed. Just thinking about him made butterflies flutter in my stomach. I looked up at him and smiled.

"What?" he said.

"Nothing." Looking into his eyes, I curled up the corner of my mouth.

"Are you flirting with me?"

"Maybe?"

He grabbed my hand and squeezed.

Closing out the parade, the firetruck passed with its sirens blasting, and the crowds began to disappear from the street.

Josh said, "I'll take Gray back to the condo and meet you at your place to help you clean and grab the last of your things."

"Okay," I said. "Take your time. Noah's coming to help, too."

Back at my apartment, we packed the last few boxes. I trotted up the steps to the bedroom loft to check and make sure I didn't leave anything up there. Noah followed closely behind. His left arm pressed against the wall, and his right arm stretched out onto the railing. I walked toward him and raised my eyebrow. "Are you going to let me pass?"

He smirked, leaning slightly closer. "That depends," he said and kissed me.

My insides instantly melted into a puddle of goo. I wrapped my arms around his neck and pulled him into me. Noah's kisses were slow and tender. He kissed my cheek and down the nape of my neck. Gripping my thighs just under my butt, he lifted me off the ground and carried me toward the bed.

Slowly, I slid down his body onto the bed. I lifted my shirt over my head, wrapped my legs around his waist, and laid back. *Thank goodness, I put on my lacy pink bra and panties this morning.*

Noah looked down at me. "Janie?"

"Yes, Noah."

"I think today is someday for me." He ran his index finger along my stomach and traced a circle around my belly button.

Confused, I said, "Umm. Okay?"

Noah chuckled. "You know... *someday* has come for me. I love you." He leaned forward and kissed my bare stomach. "I know you may not feel the same just yet. That's okay." He kissed my lips. "I'll wait for your someday, but today's mine. Actually, it's been someday for a while now." He kissed me long and hard, and I sucked in the air as his fingertips touched my cheeks. "I love you. I love being with you. I love your laugh. I love your crazy family. I love everything about you."

I smiled and slid my hands onto his ass, thrusting his hips into mine—hard. As I leaned in to kiss him, a voice suddenly called out, "Janie. I'm here."

"Shit. It's Josh." Noah jumped off me, fixed his shirt, and ran his fingers through his hair.

I hollered downstairs. "We're up here." I scrambled to put my shirt on and fix my hair.

Josh climbed the stairs, what seemed like three at a time, and said, "There's no funny business going on up here, is there?"

Noah shifted his weight. "Funny business, no sir. No funny business."

I mouthed to Noah. "Calm down. You're so obvious."

I smiled at Josh as he entered my bedroom. "We were cleaning up here. I need to move the furniture to vacuum before we leave."

Josh inhaled and looked at both of us.

Amused, I said, "All right. Let's get the dresser moved."

Noah and Josh each grabbed an end of the dresser. "On the count of three," Josh said. Something slid from behind the dresser as they scooted the heavy piece of furniture from the wall. DD squeezed her nose in the tiny space and scooped it up into her mouth before I could snatch it.

"What it is, girl? What did you find?" I tried to pry the silver item from her mouth. She snarled. DD sat on her hind legs, and her tail beat the floor frantically as she whined. Josh and Noah came over to see what was going on.

"What, DD?" Noah said. He tried to retrieve the item from her mouth.

I pet her head. "It's okay, DD. We need to see what you've got."

DD lay down and rested her head on her front paws. She let the silver item drop to the ground. Her eyes looked up at us with the sweetest puppy dog look. I reached for the item—a silver key chain. I turned it over and gasped. My hand instinctively flew to my mouth. Curious, Josh and Noah looked at me.

I turned the keychain toward them. "It says, Lizzie!" DD barked and jumped like a wild animal. "What DD? What is it?"

Her tail wagged furiously. She raised her paw, trying to bat the keychain from my hand. "Is your name Lizzie?" The dog did ten jump circles and barked excitedly. I looked at Josh and Noah.

Josh bent down on one knee and said, "Are you Lizzie?" He rubbed the top of her head.

"Do you think it's possible?" I said as DD knocked me on my back and began to lick my face. "Good girl. Sweet girl," I said as I scratched her tummy.

She ran over to Josh and rubbed her snout against his leg. "I'm not sure what's possible, but I know she's one special dog," Josh said.

EPILOGUE

Janie – Ten Years Later

Noah and I sat with little Grayson and Elizabeth as they flipped through our wedding album. Grayson was four years old and Elizabeth was three. They loved looking at our wedding photos.

"Papa Gray," Grayson said as he pointed to a picture of my father.

"Grampy Josh." Elizabeth pointed to a photo of Josh and me.

The kids favorite picture was of Josh and my father walking me down the aisle while Noah was watching. The cameraman did a great job of capturing Noah's face when he first saw me. This photo was secretly my favorite, too. The love in Noah's eyes reminds me how lucky I am to have a man like him to love and cherish for the rest of my life.

Catalina's murderer was never found.

Two years after her death, I received a letter from an attorney that she left me Bayview Books in her will. I gave half of the store to Ava, who runs the daily operations. My father passed away two weeks after the wedding, but in good old-fashioned Gray Stone style, he outlived the doctor's expectations by two years. He had many good and bad days, but it was nice to spend the last few years with him here in Southport.

I dressed Grayson in a new navy-blue suit and a purple tie. His head was full of unruly curls, but I did my best to tame them. Elizabeth wore a beautiful purple dress with ruffles. Her hair was tied into a pony tail that sprouted out of the top of her head.

Noah came into the bedroom. “You look gorgeous,” he said and kissed my cheek, making me blush, even after all these years.

Aunt Renee gave me a beautiful navy-blue gown that was my mother's. The dress had a v-cut neckline that accentuated my breasts. Made of mulberry silk, the fabric felt divine on my skin, and flowed perfectly into a mermaid cut. I buckled my silver strappy shoes and said, “You look hot yourself.”

Noah smiled. He sported a navy-blue suit and purple tie to match Grayson. DD-Lizzie was adorable, wearing a purple ring of flowers around her neck.

We entered Bayview Books through a purple and red balloon arch. Ava greeted us in a gorgeous gown. “You look fantastic,” I said.

Helen and Drew were seated on the couch.

Grayson and Elizabeth took off running. "Granny Helly and Pappy Drew," they cheered in unison. Grayson jumped into Drew's lap and clapped his hands. Elizabeth was mesmerized by Helen's diamond necklace and poked at it with her tiny fingers.

"My parents will be here in a few minutes," Ava said.

"Ava, the store looks beautiful," I said. Twinkling lights were wrapped on every railing, window, and bookcase. Vases of white lilies and red roses tied with purple ribbon sat on every table. Blue, purple, and silver balloons decorated the newel posts on the staircase and each corner of the bookstore.

Ava pointed toward the door as Josh strolled in. "Josh did most of the work."

Josh said, "Sorry I'm late. I had to run home to shower and change." DD ran toward Josh and rubbed against his leg.

I hugged him. "You did all of this?"

He smiled and nodded. "Anything for my girls."

Randy and Renee arrived a few minutes later with an enormous tower of Burney's croissants. Renee said, "They had to remake today's special, which made us a little late, sorry."

The lights around the bookstore bounced off Randy's shiny bald head. "You're looking dapper, Uncle Randy."

He smiled and rubbed his hands together. "Thanks!" Then he lifted his pant leg to show off his purple socks with white roses all over them. Renee burst out laughing.

I shook my head and smiled. "Those are perfect."

Ava guided us all to a special table set up in the center of the bookstore. A new book display was sitting on the table. The purple cover was magnificent. The title, *A Mother's Words of Wisdom* by Elizabeth Levine and Janie Miller Levine stretched across the front of the book in an embossed silver foil. White lilies and petals accented the words. I couldn't speak. I put my hands together in front of my mouth and then laid them over my heart.

Noah sniffled and said, "It's perfect."

Ava passed out glasses of champagne as we gathered around the table. Randy stood on a chair and raised his glass. "I'd like to say a few words before the crowd arrives for the official celebration. My sister was an amazing woman. We lost her too soon, but she gave life to the most extraordinary girl. Janie, your mother would be incredibly proud of you."

DD barked and raised her paw in the air.

"My sister always wanted to publish a book but didn't get to accomplish that dream. Today, we celebrate her words in conjunction with her daughter. I know this would make Lizzie happy."

Josh raised his glass, his eyes glistening and said, "Hear, hear."

Randy continued, "Janie, we're happy you're home. We love you. We love you, Noah." He tipped his glass as Grayson tugged on his pant leg. Randy picked him up and stood him on the chair beside him. "And, of course, we love you, our little Grayson man and sweet Elizabeth. Lizzie is smiling down on all of us."

DD howled and raised her paw in the air, as Josh said, "To Lizzie and Janie and their new book."

Bayview Books opened for business, and the town flooded in to celebrate the occasion with music, dancing, and shots of pirate rum.

Acknowledgments

Finishing Janie's Hope was challenging. For a large majority of the time I was dealing with health issues and the doctors couldn't figure out what was wrong. Finally, I received my diagnosis of Multiple Sclerosis and began treatment which eventually helped move me in the right direction and I was able to feel human again. At times, I struggled to type; my fingertips were in immense pain. Grateful for healing and finishing the third and final book in the Southport Series. The series has been fun to write, and I am both sad and relieved that it has come to an end. I hope that you enjoy reading the Southport Series as much as I enjoyed writing it.

I couldn't have finished the book without the help of my team, who encouraged me every step of the way. I am incredibly grateful for my amazing editors who showed tremendous grace throughout the process. Thank you, Kim, Jenn, and Adele for your kindness, intention, and hard work to help make this series come to life. You are incredible and I appreciate you.

Thank you, Mo from The Paper House for always putting up with me and my numerous cover design revisions. I appreciate your willingness to get it right.

My husband, Chris, has been my rock. He has helped me recover and heal. He held my hand when I needed it. He is my biggest cheerleader. I appreciate our time together discussing story lines, characters, and developing the plot. He is God's gift to me, and I am thankful for him every day.

My children think it's cool that their mom writes books, and my daughter is my best salesman. Thank you for putting up with Mom's late-night and weekend writing sessions. I love you both to the moon and back.

I must acknowledge my college roommate Steph, who is by my side and cheers me on every step of the way. She will read draft and after draft and provide honest, constructive feedback. She also reminds me to keep going when I begin to doubt myself.

My launch team is tremendous. There are almost one hundred members,, and they know who they are. Marketing the Southport Series was a three-book commitment, and they rocked. Thank you for your time, effort, and support.

Last but definitely not least, I thank my family and friends for supporting and rooting for me. I am grateful to you. I could not do this without your love and encouragement. I love you all.

From The Author

Several years ago, I decided I wanted to be a writer. I started my debut novel, The Secrets We Conceal, a coming-of-age fiction based on a true story. After releasing the book and deciding to write another, I needed time to figure out my next story.

I was going through some personal difficulties, struggling to find gratitude each day. My siblings are a huge part of my life, but I rarely see them because we live in different states. I decided I needed to take a trip to visit, and I did. Spending time surrounded by the comfort and love of my brother and sister was exactly what I needed to get back on track. Enjoying the beautiful weather and the small town of Southport, NC, catapulted me into a story, and I couldn't move my fingers fast enough to write it. I sat at a picnic table on the water, whipped out an outline, and feverishly developed the characters and plot. The process was exhilarating, and Call Her Janie was born.

Not long after starting Call Her Janie, I knew the book needed to be a series, and Keeping Janie came to life. Janie's Hope is now finished, and the trilogy is complete.

Everyone should have someone they can lean on to lift their spirits and help them find the strength they need to get through anything. In the Southport Series, Lizzie leans on her brother and Helen to lift her up and find her way. I hope you enjoy the Series as much as I enjoyed writing it.

Do you have a story to tell? Would you like me to join your book club to discuss my books? I'm happy to join your book club or help you tell your own story. Reach out any time to srfabricoauthor@gmail.com. If you feel compelled, please leave an honest review on Goodreads, Amazon, or anywhere books are sold.

Book Club Questions

1. Which character did you connect with most? Why?
2. Do you agree with how Gray raised Janie? What would you have done differently?
3. Did you enjoy how the book ended? What would be another option?
4. Were you glad that Catalina finally got what was coming to her?
5. Do you think DD was Lizzie?
6. What surprised you?
7. What was your favorite scene?
8. How did the Southport Series make you feel?
9. How did the author's writing style impact the story?
10. If you could ask the author one question, what would it be?

About the Author

S.R. Fabrico is a multi-award-winning author whose literary talents have captivated readers worldwide. With her debut novel, The Secrets We Conceal, and her second novel, Call Her Janie, she has emerged as a rising star in the literary realm.

With a remarkable 25-plus-year career in business, marketing, and sports, S.R. Fabrico brings a unique perspective to her writing. As a World Champion Dance Coach and esteemed speaker, she infuses her stories with passion and insight.

Residing in Tennessee with her husband and children, S.R. Fabrico continues to create captivating narratives that will transport you to new and extraordinary worlds. Prepare to be enchanted by her exceptional storytelling prowess.

In addition to her passion for writing novels, she has published a series of sports journals and a journal for women. She believes that journaling is good for the soul.

Also by S.R. Fabrico

Connect with S.R. Fabrico

Subscribe and follow S.R. Fabrico to stay up to date on new releases and important update.

Email srfabricoauthor@gmail.com to set up a virtual or in person book club meet and greet with the author.

Made in USA - Kendallville, IN
39745_9781962546072
01.07.2025 2156